ROUX THE BANDIT

ROUX THE BANDIT

by
André Chamson

Translated by
Van Wyck Brooks

C
CASEMATE
uk
Oxford & Philadelphia

Published in Great Britain and
the United States of America in 2016 by
CASEMATE PUBLISHERS
10 Hythe Bridge Street, Oxford OX1 2EW, UK
and
1950 Lawrence Road, Havertown, PA 19083, USA

Roux le Bandit © André Chamson 1938
Introduction Lawrence Brown © Casemate UK, 2016

Paperback Edition: ISBN 978-1-61200-417-4
Digital Edition: ISBN 978-1-61200-418-1 (epub)

A CIP record for this book is available from the British Library

Printed in the Czech Republic by FINIDR

For a complete list of Casemate titles, please contact:

CASEMATE PUBLISHERS (UK)
Telephone (01865) 241249
Fax (01865) 794449
Email: casemate-uk@casematepublishers.co.uk
www.casematepublishers.co.uk

CASEMATE PUBLISHERS (US)
Telephone (610) 853-9131
Fax (610) 853-9146
Email: casemate@casematepublishing.com
www.casematepublishing.com

CONTENTS

A MON FRÈRE

The Cévenols make good soldiers,
and are well qualified for war
and for service in the infantry.
          —*Memoirs of Basville.*

INTRODUCTION

I N 1914, rural France was as far removed from the bustling cities as we are today from the world that existed before the First World War broke out. The world in which Roux lived was one where people went about their daily existence in the same way as their forebears had before and since the Revolution. With the arrival of summer, well-heeled Parisians set off for the coastal resorts of Deauville or south towards Nice and Cannes, along new rail networks in first-class coaches shining with mahogany fittings and Limoges porcelain. The other France, that of the country, took ancient tools and began the task of collecting the crops.

Indeed, France in the early 20th century could be defined as being mostly rural with only 44% of the population of 42 million living in urban areas according to the census of 1911. Thus, 40% of the active population was involved in agriculture, fishing or forestry. The various regions of France had strong cultural identities and in many cases spoke in local dialects rather than French. The rural populations were not very mobile and, in mountainous areas especially, there was little contact with the outside world. News would be passed on in the village café, or pasted onto the noticeboard of the *mairie* that even the smallest village possessed.

A new annual event might have brought a taste of the modern world which lay beyond to these remote areas – a procession of dust-covered convicts of the road, toiling up mountain tracks on heavy bicycles and followed by cars carrying men in tweed suits. The pioneers of the Tour de

France were hard men and the race was three weeks of hard labour, something to which the men and women of rural France could relate. Cyclists became national heroes and in urban areas the sport became a thriving pastime. The heroes of the Tour gained national fame, men such as Lucien Petit-Breton, Octave Lapize and François Faber ... all of whom fell in the war.

Another reality for people such as Roux was that of the *école républicaine* and national military service. A law rendering obligatory secular education between the ages of six and 13 was passed in 1882. It was in this environment that the idea of duty to the nation was instilled and also the notion of revenge for the loss of the Alsace and Lorraine regions to the Prussians following the disastrous and costly war of 1870–71. Despite this, many of the more remote areas remained closely attached to the church, despite the separation of the latter and the state in 1905. There was a certain apprehension towards military matters; after all, it was only a century since Napoleon had caused such demographic damage with his campaigns. However, on the eve of war, three years' military service was compulsory and it was through the fulfilment of this obligation that rural and urban populations mixed and were imbued further with the notion of duty towards the motherland, especially in view of the increasing bellicosity of their neighbour across the Rhine. Once released from his military service, a man would remain liable to be called up as a reservist.

Following the events in Sarajevo on 28 June 1914, life went on the same as it always had. Indeed, in rural areas the assassination of Austrian Archduke Franz Ferdinand and his wife would have barely raised an eyebrow. In the towns and cities, attention was focused on the political scandal and trial of Henriette Caillaux, the wife of the Minister of Finance, Joseph Caillaux. On 20 July 1914, Madame Caillaux stood trial for the murder of *Le Figaro* newspaper journalist and chief editor, Gaston Calmette. Joseph Cailloux had been the subject of a campaign, led by *Le Figaro*, accusing him of corruption. His wife, exasperated and exhausted by this three-month campaign, purchased a pistol and went to the newspaper's offices where she confronted and shot Calmette. The trial was on the front pages of regional and national newspapers, overshadowing the dark clouds gathering on the geo-political stage. Pleading a crime of passion, Madame Caillaux was acquitted on 28 July, the day on which Austria declared war on Serbia and set the dominos tumbling.

France, along with other countries, at last woke up to the possibility of a European war. On 31 July, Jean Jaurès, a leading pacifist and socialist politician, attempted to halt the impending clash of arms. After having written an article for his newspaper *l'Humanité* he went to a café where he was shot by a pro-war nationalist. Paradoxically, his death led to socialists rallying to the *Union Sacrée* of national unity. On 2 August, mobilisation posters were placed in village squares and on town halls. Church bells rang out across fields and valleys, calling men from their occupations; many of them would be in combat within three weeks. It is often said that the men were happy to go, after all this is what the nation had prepared them for since their school days and military service. However, in rural communities the men left behind the ripening crops – who would deal with the harvest?

The men of Roux's rural community liable to be called up as reservists – aged between 24 and 34 years of age – would make their way to the barracks, which were usually situated in larger towns. Once there, many men were met with scenes of chaos as the regular regiments were marched away. Reserve regiments were formed on the basis of the regular units. Many of the reserve regiments were left with second-rate equipment and uniforms but were mostly ready to move out by 5 August. The French army was organised into 22 military regions with each one capable of raising an army corps comprising several divisions. Like the Germans' Schlieffen Plan, the French had devised their own, the ill-fated Plan XVII which comprised of a rapid mobilisation and attack into the lost regions of Alsace and Lorraine. However, given the German plan of attack, this was akin to placing their head in a noose. The archaic nature of the plan of attack was matched by that of the uniforms; men were sent into battle wearing dark greatcoats and *garance* red trousers that harked back to Napoleonic times.

Back in the villages, towns and cities, events were followed with great passion. This time the hated Boches would be defeated and France would regain its honour and lost provinces. There would have been little sympathy for deserters or shirkers. Men who had not shown up on the day their mobilisation cards stipulated could expect the gendarmes to knock on their door and forcibly escort them to the barracks. Those who were not at home were deemed as having deserted and thus liable to the full force of military law; moreover, they could not rely on any help from their communities.

The French plan of action took men from all corners of France by train towards the border with Germany. A French priest, Jean Bouysonnie from Périgueux, called up as a stretcher-bearer, recalled seeing the men pointing excitedly as their train passed through the outskirts of Paris, enthralled as they saw the capital for the first time in their lives. As elsewhere, they were all told it would be over by Christmas. Fighting began as early as 7 August with small-scale clashes along the border. However, this soon intensified into a series of battles known as the *bataille des frontières* and losses mounted. Fighting on 22 August 1914 cost the French army a staggering 27,000 men killed in action. The French, supported by the small British Expeditionary Force, began to fall back. On 27 August, the men of the rural reserve *338e régiment d'infanterie*, from the Limousin, awaited the Germans in the rolling Picardy countryside astride the main road leading south towards Paris. Within a couple of hours they were massacred by an enemy shrouded in morning fog – more than 700 men would not return to their villages.

Despite the appalling losses of the first four months of the war – almost a million casualties – there was still an overall feeling that the men had fallen gloriously for a noble cause in defending their homeland, even if the northern parts

11

of France were essentially foreign to the rural population of regions such as the Cévennes, where the novel is set. The dead were eulogised in their communities and in the newspapers. However, it could be argued that an anti-war sentiment came relatively early to France. Hundreds of villages and towns were hit with heavy losses in the early days of the war, locally raised regiments such as the *338e RI* were wiped out and the local gendarmes were kept busy informing families of their losses. In Britain this would come later; while the small BEF also lost many men, these were mostly professional soldiers doing their duty, albeit nobly and honoured by their country.

As 1914 came to a close, the Western Front had settled into siege warfare along over 700 kilometres of trench lines from the North Sea to Switzerland. Moreover, six French departments, including the industrial heartland of the north, were under partial or total German occupation. This was exploited by the French press, especially the brutality of the Germans in the opening phase of the war. The German approach to the occupied areas was one of domination based on fear. In the Nord department, the second largest industrial zone after Paris, factories and mines were requisitioned, and machinery dismantled and taken to Germany. Agricultural sectors were also affected with the confiscation of livestock and crops making food scarce for the local population. The latter were also used as a source of labour by the Germans.

It was not surprising, therefore that truces, such as those held between the British and Germans near Ypres and

Armentières at Christmas 1914, were not as widespread on sections of the front line held by the French. There were cases of temporary cessations of hostilities but the French attitude towards their enemy had not softened, they were still very much the invader. This attitude would change as the war progressed and front-line soldiers felt a sort of brotherhood of common suffering with their German counterparts.

The year 1915 saw France take a resolutely offensive stance. According to their commander-in-chief, Général Joffre, the French army would nibble away at the German lines before breaking through and pushing out the invader. The problem was that artillery was not yet powerful enough to crush defences and neutralise enemy fire. This second year of the war was, therefore, extremely costly to the French; indeed, in this grim parade of death, 1915 takes the front of the procession with 349,000 killed. People at home, especially in more remote regions where news took time to filter through, were not yet aware of the scale of losses nationwide. The French military high command did not communicate its losses to a government which, in any case, was keen to stifle such terrible statistics in order to maintain national morale. Moreover, the French army was unable to keep track of its losses and many men killed in action were simply registered as missing. Thus families continued to hope that their missing loved ones had been taken prisoner. The first of the 1915 offensives took place in the Artois region around Arras (March–May 1915), in which the British played a comparatively minor role.

Gas was unleashed on the French in the Ypres region on 22 April and this new development in industrial warfare was decried as yet another example of a barbaric enemy. Further attacks were launched in September, in the Lens region and Champagne, but resulted in nothing more than adding to the grisly pyre.

At the end of the first full year of war the trench lines had barely moved and success, if any, was measured in metres rather than kilometres. Joffre, imperturbable and calm as ever, saw this as part of a necessary wearing-down process. However, for the front-line infantryman this was nothing more than a futile waste of life; he had no concept of strategy and even less so of tactics, which if there were any, soon fell apart against the grim reality of German bullets and shells. French military justice was extremely brutal and would reach such levels that it took parliamentary intervention to rein in the martial ardour and expedient methods of regimental and divisional commanders. One such example is that of the *63ème régiment d'infanterie* of Limoges involved in the grim fighting in the Flirey sector of the Lorraine. Exhausted from countless attacks, the men had no more to give and refused to attack yet again. The general commanding the corps took the extraordinary decision to court martial an entire company. A compromise of sorts was reached with four men chosen for execution. However, those chosen were known for pre-war membership of the CGT trade union . . . something seen as threat to the ruling classes. After the most basic of trials on 19 April, the four were shot the next day. Such injustices did reach the ears of civilians via letters that escaped the eyes of the censors; diaries also told tales of such travesties where the men of the regiments involved were forced to witness the executions and then marched past the poles against which slumped the limp bodies of their comrades. All of this was sowing bitter seeds that would yield deadly fruit in 1917. The end of 1915 also saw a major inter-Allied conference held at Chantilly. It was decided to undertake a series of offensives on such a scale that the Germans and their allies, hit on all fronts, would have no option but to sue for peace. It was hoped that the British and Empire forces would be able to take more of the burden. Indeed, the junior ally was increasingly taking over parts of the front line, and the volunteers of Kitchener's Army were arriving in larger numbers. They would be able to play a part in the forthcoming offensives, despite the fact that the French military viewed them with some disdain, seeing them as nothing more than amateurs led by amateurs.

For the French, 1916 was the year of Verdun, a titanic struggle for national survival that overshadowed everything else. Blissfully unaware of Allied plans to attack in 1916, it was the Germans who struck first at Verdun, a small town on the banks of the river Meuse and one of great symbolic, rather than strategic value. It was in Verdun, in the year 843 that Charlemagne's great empire was split into three in a treaty that many historians consider as being the foundation of France and Germany. It was at Verdun that the war became truly industrial; the might of the Krupp factories poured a storm of steel onto the French defenders. Verdun became a mincing machine through which virtually every French infantry regiment passed. The nation shuddered at the loss of the jewel in the crown of the French defences, Fort Douaumont, and other names, such as Fleury, Vaux, Côte 304 and Mort-Homme gained national and worldwide notoriety as the French clung on in the face of the German onslaught. The battle rallied France once more behind the war effort. This was not a time for political cleavage, but rather one of *union sacrée* as had been the case in 1914. Towns and villages all over France renamed squares and streets in honour of the fighting at Verdun. The battle would eventually come to a halt in December 1916 with the French back to their original front line. They had held on against the industrial might of Germany, but had been left exhausted and spent.

1916 was also the year of the Somme, an offensive planned in December 1915 at Chantilly as a joint Franco-British attack. There was not much to be gained strategically, no major town, nor any main railway lines used by the Germans as a vital means of transferring supplies and reserves from one end of the Western Front to the other. For the French, however, it was the point where the two Allied armies met and they could, therefore, keep an eye on their junior and *amateur* partner.

The attack at Verdun threw plans into disarray with the initial French contribution greatly reduced. However, the attack was now essential in order to draw away German reserves from Verdun. The British losses on the first day of the attack are well known and documented; what is less well known is that the French attack, just north of, but mainly to the south of the Somme river, across the Santerre plateau was a great success. It could be argued that topography offered fewer challenges, but moreover, the French were able to draw upon experience that the British had yet to gain. Unlike the extended lines of advancing infantry of the British, the French used fire and movement tactics and could call upon heavy artillery (which the British did not have in sufficient numbers), in order to neutralise German defences. Indeed, it is quite remarkable that France, given its lower industrial output prior to the war, was capable of producing prodigious quantities of war *matériel* and this is even more notable when one considers that much of its ore-producing and heavy industry sectors were under enemy occupation.

As in Britain and Germany, women were mobilised on a massive scale to play a vital role in the war effort. This was not only in the fields, but also in the factories, driving trams, and many other occupations that had previously been seen as exclusively masculine. As in many countries, there had been a suffragette movement in France before the war. In 1909, Jeanne-Elizabeth Schmahl established the French Union for Women's Suffrage but by 1916, the majority of French women were too busy working in exhausting jobs, grieving or apprehending the knock on the door to be worried about the right to vote.

Attitudes towards the war were perhaps beginning to change towards the end of 1916. The work of Henri Barbusse and his famous novel, *Le Feu*, at first serialised, woke people up to the brutal realities of the war, hitherto hidden behind censorship and glorified imagery. Published in November 1916 and widely read, the novel marked a change in public perception of the war. This led to a sharp increase in charitable institutions sending gifts and comforts to the men at the front, as well as a movement of *marraines de guerre*, women who adopted a soldier and sent them correspondence, food and other comforts.

The soldiers' perception of civilians, however, was somewhat different. If a soldier was lucky enough to obtain a short period of leave, he could be standing on a Parisian train platform within half a day, still caked in the damp mud of the Aisne or the Somme. He was no longer met by a euphoric and grateful crowd but rather a sullen indifference. In Paris, where the sound of artillery fire could be clearly heard when carried on a favourable wind, the well-connected could still enjoy an expensive meal or a music-hall show. It was a world of rear-echelon officers wearing tailor-made uniforms and service chevrons earned not in the misery of mud-filled trenches, but in comfortable offices where the only weapons were fountain pens. The gulf between the combatant and the rear was huge. The fighting men, of a caste created in the cauldron of battle, formed unions after the war and fiercely protected their status as *anciens combattants*.

The year 1917 was marked by a surprise German tactical withdrawal to a new defensive position, the Hindenburg Line. This was born of necessity, the German army had been badly mauled in the twin battles of the Somme and by thus withdrawing, was able to shorten the front line and free up reserves. In so doing, the Germans undertook a scorched-earth policy, leaving nothing behind that might have been of use to the advancing Allies. This left a strong and lasting impression on the French soldiers, who had become used to the sight of destroyed buildings but who were scandalized by the deliberate felling of orchards and the poisoning of wells. Men were also shocked at the pitiful state of liberated civilians, reduced to exhausted subjugation by the occupying forces. All of these factors were used to great effect by the propaganda services and helped bolster national resolve in the face of a creeping war weariness.

Once again the campaign season was afoot. Plans had been drawn up for a joint spring offensive. The new French commander-in-chief, Robert Nivelle, whose star had risen at Verdun, wanted to attack the German-held heights above the river Aisne along the Chemin des Dames. The British would attack at Arras in a diversionary role, drawing away German reserves before the French struck. The British and Empire forces met with initial success before the attack broke down into the traditional stalemate of attritional and static warfare. The French attacked a week later on 16 April 1917. It was, even given the previous failures, an unmitigated disaster. Heralded by Nivelle as the attack that would lead to a breakthrough and the end of the war, the French were massacred. Instead of calling off the attack, Nivelle decided to continue, but the men could do no more. The subsequent crisis is more often described as a mutiny, it was, however, more akin to a series of strikes. The exhausted French army saw units refuse to be wasted in such futile and costly attacks; they would die for France but not for a general desperate for some ardent glory.

The French army did what it could to stifle the events; court martials were held and over fifty of the most militant ringleaders were shot. The French military and government were terrified of a Bolshevik-type uprising which, in light of events in Russia, was a genuine source of fear to the establishment. Offensive action for the remainder of the year was off the cards, they would now wait for the Americans, who had declared war on 6 April, but who would not be ready for offensive action until well into 1918. Measures were taken to try and improve life for the front-line soldier; the system of leave was made more equitable and food was improved. The burden of continuing the war on the Western Front for the rest of the year mostly fell, in terms of offensive action, to the British and Empire divisions.

In 1918 the war, albeit in a relatively minor way, really reached Paris. They had, in the same way as British cities, suffered the odd Zeppelin raid but in 1918 the capital city was within reach of a new long-range artillery gun hidden in the St. Gobain forest. Death would fall out of nowhere and without warning, akin to the V2 rockets that fell on Britain in the Second World War. Hundreds of shells hit the city, reaching a climax on 29 March when the St. Gervais church was hit, causing the roof to collapse and killing 88 people. Gotha bombers were also increasingly a source of death and destruction. Civilians became increasingly superstitious and took to wearing two small lucky charms named Rintintin and Nenette. Morale was also rattled by a series of German offensives. The collapse and subsequent surrender of the Russians on the Eastern Front freed up a vast quantity of men and guns. The Germans knew that they had to unleash their forces in one last roll of the dice before the Americans arrived in sufficient numbers to tip the balance in the Allies' favour. The first of these attacks was against a weakened and over-extended part of the front line held by the British. As the German tide swept forward a conference was held in Doullens and the decision was taken to name Foch as the supreme Allied commander. Further German attacks were launched against French-held sectors and at one point it looked as though Paris itself would be threatened. However, the Germans had shot their bolt and the Allies rallied, launching a series of counter-offensives in July and August that pushed the enemy back towards the border.

The end of the war brought demobilisation for millions of men and women. Those who hailed from regions through which the war had passed faced years of precarious living in temporary housing or even former dugouts. On the former battlefields they would live with the detritus of war, as they still do to some extent today. The hard-working French peasant returned to areas, such as the Somme, so vital to France's food requirements and stolidly set to work filling in shell holes and trench lines in order that crops flourish once more. Towns and villages grew used to the sight of the mutilated, not only in body but also in spirit.

As for deserters such as Roux, the war was not over as the French Gendarmerie continued to track them down. It is highly unlikely that the civilian population would have been overly sympathetic to their plight and the returning servicemen would have been even less forgiving. A certain understanding would come later with the advent of pacifist views and literature. Only 1.5% of French men deserted upon mobilisation in August 1914 but this number increased as the war went on and young conscripts became increasingly aware of the realities of the war. Statistics show 15,600 desertions in 1916 and 25,579 the following year. The penalties were severe; prison and forced labour or death. This meant that many felt they had nothing to lose in the event of arrest – there were many cases of gendarmes being shot. Most of France shunned deserters and they had little option but to turn to banditry and robbery as a means of subsistence. Some regions of France, such as Corsica, the Ardeche and the Pyrenees, traditionally less amenable to state intervention, were less hostile and even active in helping hide deserters; indeed many crossed the border into Spain to find refuge, but the gendarmes were often waiting for them many years after the war ended. The official hunt and punishment of deserters did not cease until 1928.

Lawrence Brown

PROLOGUE

THE usury of the earth has mastered the pride of the mountains. The lines of peaks incline gently toward one another and unite through the open notches of the hills. From one notch to another, over the shorn grass and the thistles, the uplands seem vainly to seek some limit in space, and every hillock reveals a circular horizon as vast as that of the sea.

Three cold springs that meet on these uncertain slopes and give way suddenly in cascades on a rocky lip of the plateau have hollowed out the valley.

From the highest zigzag of the road that leads us to the village, before entering the narrow shade of the houses, we can see it all, from the two mills of La Bessède as far as the notch of the Pas and the equal peaks of the Aire de Côte.

These mountains—in spite of their uncultivated slopes and their long stone ridges—are not inhuman, for, with a certain foresight and resigned tenacity, one can live there. But while even the highest altitudes permit of houses or villages, they restrict them to exact and limited spots and, while imposing upon them a semi-solitude, welcome them as if with a certain reservation.

The people who live here have accepted still more rigorous inner laws; they respond as scrupulous and wilful masters to the problems that life poses to them and yet their everyday occupations are so severe and so imperious that men of less heroism would gradually lose there the sense of their souls.

They cultivate vines, olives, mulberries, in the lower parts of their domain, and these are the works they delight in, but they also plough the earth for rye, in the long, undulating bands on the mid-slope of the mountain, and cut down the fir-trees and the beeches on the borders of the pastures where the custody of the flocks goes on for ever.

A destiny of security and solitude, an annual cycle of abundance and harsh struggle attaches them to their mountains. They live on olives and grapes, on ears of rye and off the forest.

They are peasants of France, but I do not wish to imply that I have collected their words and reported their acts in an attempt to determine any of the characters of this earthy race, whose spiritual unity or even its general tendencies I only perceive in rare historic sublimations, not in the course of daily and direct experiences.

I cannot see in them anything but peasants of a certain region of France, and their deeds and their conversation do not seem to me necessarily to represent the consciousness of the vintners of the neighbouring plain, or that of the labourers in the valleys and the hills scattered along the brooks and rivers about the mountains where they dwell.

These mountaineers of the Cévennes obey moral laws that are all their own, but this circumstance does not seem to me to isolate them from the world or to diminish the value of their testimony. I believe, on the contrary, that the forces that bring them close to other men are more resistant and more lasting than those that unite in the national consciousness.

They are born from that narrow but profound experience of life, from that severe but incontestable dignity which is conferred by daily work on the land more than by any other labour; they have drawn their richness from the age-old permanence of a state of culture and equilibrium that has endured for generations, and perhaps from a heart-felt attachment to the early teachings of Christianity.

This simplicity undoubtedly unites these men to all Europe—to the spiritual unity of Europe, and perhaps even to other continents than ours. One must always feel in connection with them this long train of natural affinities which I have thought myself bound to suggest before letting them speak for themselves. . . .

But at the very moment when I reach the end of this research, a still more imperious obligation urges me to say that there is no country which can give them a more evident and more harmonious relationship than that which France has reserved for them: mountaineers of the Alpine, Pyrenean, and Breton valleys, Ardennais, perhaps, men of Morvan and from the valleys and high pastures of the Juras.

We had spent the night walking on the mountain.

When dawn came, cold and sudden, we had lain in hiding before the mysterious line of the fir-groves and all the morning we had beat about for wild boars in the bogs, which were full of springs. . . . When a beast was killed we slung it between two beech branches, and bearing the

We slung it between two beech branches.

branches on our shoulders with the crucified and bleeding animal we climbed down to the village.

The women had taken advantage of the hunting day to go down to the market in the town. We were alone, masters of our pleasures and our rest.

In spite of the mildness of the autumn and especially of the afternoon that lingered on for a long time in the naked air and over the pavement of the terrace, tired from the hunt and the long hours out of doors we had lighted a fire as a symbol of fatigue and tranquillity.

ROUX THE BANDIT

I

"Roux, he is the man who has done time. In the country everybody calls him Roux the Bandit, and I can't give him any other name now, I'm so used to it. But, just the same, if he were here, I'd be happy and proud to shake his hand."

The listeners approved. . . . All these men of the mountain evidently knew the story of Roux the Bandit. . . . They had undoubtedly heard it many times already, but on this afternoon of rest they were all willing to hear it once more, and they even lent it the respectful and passionate attention which they could give only to symbolic events.

Their attention manifested in advance the moral value of this story; for, Cévenols of the valley or the mountain, ardently submissive to the discipline of the sacred parables, voluntarily poor in tales and local legends, occupied solely with biblical memories and with a few stories of confessors and martyrs who revived and eternised them, they were unable to be deeply interested in a simple romantic story. When they fastened upon some legend, it was always because they found in it a moral teaching, a logical continuation of the gospels, a sermon that had been lived and upon which they could meditate and argue, as they loved to do with the verses of the Bible.

There is something in this tendency that recalls the Roman custom of the gloss, and these simple keepers of goats and cattle, these thick-set labourers of the north of Gard, make me think of the subtle doctors of the Middle Ages, who carried on unceasingly a debate on the fundamentals of problems without thinking of giving them a new form.

Finiels went on: "We all know him, for he came from Sauveplane, the last farm of our valley toward the mountain. . . . You will find this farm on the left hand, going up to Luzette, beyond the big fields of the estate of Puéchagut. It is just on the border of the chestnut woods, beside a good spring where you will find the only three poplars of this mountain. Roux lived there, with his mother and his two sisters. He had some property of his own, and his father left him enough to see him through the winters without anxiety if he worked hard. He had this farm, a few vines and a few mulberry-trees over by the valley, and a pasture for his beasts on the mountain. But at Sauveplane the winter is hard, and during the bad season you can do nothing, so that the vines, the beasts, and the few fields of rye, were not enough work for this boy, especially since his two sisters and his mother took charge of the animals and all the work on the farm. So Roux worked most of all on the mountain, in the State woods, where he bought trees to cut down: he did his heaviest work there, and that was the best part of his trade. On the mountain he cut his wood, made up his bundles of faggots, loaded them on his cart and then, when the weather was fine, when the forest roads were firm, he carted them to the station with his pair of oxen, which before the war were worth all of a thousand francs. . . . In the good season, he spent every week here: my boy would whistle to him as he went by and go down with him as far as Saint-Jean. They had been to school together and taken their diplomas the same year, and it was always a pleasure to them to meet again for a little."

This detail snatched Roux the Bandit out of his legendary setting. I had thought I divined in him some half-fabulous personage of the ancient local legends. He revealed himself, on the contrary, as a young man like the "boy" who, standing beside me, nodded in approval of his father's words. . . .

Thirty-five years old, short in stature but solid, a peasant from his childhood, a product of the elementary school and of wild rambles over the countryside, used to animals— horses or cattle—accustomed to tools and accustomed to the soil. But beneath this completely peasant appearance, you divined the marks of another existence, the long habit of another service than that of the earth, the harsh experience of servitudes harder still than those of labour, of a parsimonious and always anxious life, and of the semi-solitude of the mountain.

Looking at the son of Finiels and the other mountaineers who surrounded us, I replaced Roux amid his fellows and, thanks to these men, I could imagine him clearly and form a good idea of his manner of life. . . . The vagabond childhood in the narrow circle of a valley between two lines of mountains: the care of the beasts, the search for mushrooms, the carting of dry wood, the gathering of chestnuts and grapes; the general gravity of this childhood, the daily spectacle of the stern peaks and sad valleys, the poverty of the landscape and of the villages and the houses; the river, the highway, the four roads, the thousand paths of the mountains; the austerity of the old people, their authority over everything, the teaching of the home, more dogmatic than that of the school; the religious traditions, the custom of sermons and prayers, the observance of the great rules of Christian morality envisaged with a cold, Protestant, and mountaineer resolution. . . . Then suddenly, in the midst of these customs, these traditions, this material and moral solitude, the war: and the five years of service, the fatigues and the dangers, the life of war learned as a second trade.

Finiels went on: "On Sunday he would go down to Saint-Jean with his mother and his two sisters for the afternoon service. He could not go to the morning service because of the distance, but he always arranged to have dinner early and to go and be present at the service in the great meeting-house or at the Methodist chapel. He went more often to the chapel, by preference, having nothing in common with those pillars of the Church who seek above everything to make themselves seen and to insinuate themselves everywhere. He was a straightforward boy who enjoyed hearing the word of God, and although he did not attend all the prayer meetings and all the services, he knew his Bible and respected good morals.

"I would have answered for him as for my own boy and even more so, for he had never been foolish. He paid no attention to the girls, and although he drank his wine heartily nobody ever saw him take a drop too much. . . .

"To sum it all up, he was a little shy, a little aloof, and I don't think people saw him laugh very often. He also had an air of severity and a sort of natural pride that kept him from talking to people whom he did not know very well, but if he lived a good deal within himself that was because of the mountain life and the habit of his trade as a woodcutter which left him entirely alone for days at a time, and not because of ill nature or malice.

"Things were drifting along in their usual way when the war came. You know how it caught us: people had been discussing it for many days when, on Saturday, the mobilisation was announced. We all went down to Saint-Jean as if we were going to market and betook ourselves to the Town Hall. There we found the public notices. Drums were beating and the bells of the church and the Protestant chapel were pealing.

"I met Roux on the square, with all the others: the young people were singing, the women were weeping, and we old folks were concerning ourselves for the crops, the live-stock, the houses, and other property of the families. . . . Amid this confusion the mayor passed and shouted to me:

" 'Your boy is going off, Finiels, but mobilisation isn't war. They'll be afraid at the last moment when they see that we are ready.'

" 'Of course they will,' I said to him. 'Of course they will.'

" 'If nobody were willing to go to war,' said Roux to me, 'it would be still more certain.'

"My blood boiled and I lost my temper.

" 'Would you rather stay behind and let the others go in your place?'

" 'What I wish is that men wouldn't kill one another.'

"Just then my boy, who was passing with a group of young men, called out:

" 'Well, Roux, so we are going off together?'

"But Roux began quoting Scripture and making a sort of sermon on war and on righteousness. All around us the young men listened to him. But this was not a day for patience. They called to him:

" 'So you'd like them to come here and take your farm and your sisters and your mother away from you?'

"Everybody knew Roux. They were all his friends, but for a moment I thought they were going to give him a bad time of it.

" 'You're talking nonsense,' I said to him, and thereupon we ended the conversation and went up to the farm to get the boy's bundles ready.

"Roux went up with us and did not open his mouth the whole way. When we arrived he left us and went on his way to Sauveplane.

" 'See you soon,' my boy shouted to him.

"Roux turned around and made a gesture with his arms, like this, as if to say 'au revoir,' and was gone.

"We made up the bundles, the accounts, everything that had to be done, and went down with the boy to the station. . . . You know Saint-Jean: it is just one long narrow street, so small that the tradesfolk have only to come out on their doorsteps for the town to seem full of people. The square they have made at the end of the street, just this side of the station, is scarcely larger, and the boys and girls almost fill it on summer evenings when they come in bands to wait for the ten o'clock train. . . . But this day was indeed the greatest day that people had ever seen in this place. The townsfolk, the people of the three valleys, and even those from the mountain were all there together. . . . We looked for Roux in this crowd, I asked everybody for news of him. Nobody had seen Roux of Sauveplane.

" 'I'll find him again at Nîmes,' said my boy. 'He has followed the short cuts down and ought to be in the train already.'

"After this we thought no more of Roux. . . . You understand that we had plenty of other things to talk about.

"When my son was gone, I went up to the farm again. There was no lack of work to be done there. . . . The young men had left us all alone for the heavy work of the summer: on the hills the harvest was not yet entirely in, and down in the valley bottoms it was already time to think of gathering the grapes.

"Some time afterward, I was in my terraced garden above the road, when the police-sergeant from Saint-Jean passed with a *gendarme*.

" 'Good day, Finiels.'

" 'Good day, gentlemen.'

"I came down from my terraces and asked them if they were going up to Sauveplane.

35

"This was no sort of question to ask them, for by this road you can go only to Sauveplane or to the mountain, and surely I thought that at that season there was nothing to take the *gendarmes* to the mountain.

" 'Exactly,' the police-sergeant replied. 'Roux has not signed up. We are going to see if he is at his farm.'

"I thought of my son who had left us without news for two weeks, and anger seized me. I began to say: 'The monster . . .' The sergeant answered:

" 'He is a deserter.'

"Deserter? That is not a word that means anything to us. It is a school-teacher's word, a school-book word. I said to the sergeant:

" 'Deserter, if you wish, that is quite possible; but he is a monster.'

"The sergeant, who was not from this neighbourhood, looked at me stupidly, then he replied:

" 'Exactly, he is a deserter.'

"But as for me, I repeated in patois to the sergeant who understood me very well, since he has been in the canton for more than ten years: '*D'aquéu mounstre, aï, d'aquéu mounstre.*' After a moment the sergeant asked me with an air of embarrassment:

" 'There is nobody at Sauveplane but his mother and his sisters?'

" 'So far as I can tell you.'

"I reflected a moment, then added:

" 'If you wish me to go with you, I am your man. I know the family and the ways of the house.'

" 'Come along then, Finiels, you can speak to these women. You will frighten them less than we would.'

" 'Of course we are neighbours, and in a way it is doing them a kindness.'

"Saying this, I took my jacket and we went up together.

"It is our custom to have a finger in everything that goes on at Sauveplane, and the people of Sauveplane do the same with us. It has been so from old times, and of necessity because of our solitude: let a misfortune happen at Sauveplane and we go up there at once, and when something happens to us down come the people from up there.

"The first time I went up to Sauveplane it was with my grandfather, when I was not yet eight years old, and because of an accident that had befallen Roux's great-grandfather. While cutting down his wood, he had been bitten by a snake, in his side, through his shirt.

"At this time, there was another family at Sauveplane, who lived in the abandoned hut beside the spring.... Since then, these people have fallen on hard times, they have gone off to die in the towns, and the daughter has ended by selling herself to men for a trifle. That day this same girl came running down crying:

" 'Roux has been bitten by some poisonous creature.'

"My grandfather, who knew a lot about plants and remedies, took his jacket and called to me:

" 'Come with me; you can come back and get things if necessary.'

"And I set out with my grandfather. We reached Sauveplane: the old man lay on the straw, in front of his door, all blue and puffed up like a toad, with his shirt unbuttoned and a great wound in his side. The women had burned it with a red-hot iron, but too late, for he had been twenty minutes running home with the creature's poison under his skin. He was already losing consciousness. My grandfather looked at him and said to me:

" 'Go down to the farm and tell your father to come up and tell the women not to wait for us this evening.'

"Of course he was already thinking of putting the dead man in his shroud and watching beside him. . . . So I took the road down and came back alone from Sauveplane for the first time, which was not very difficult since there was only one road that always followed the course of the valley. . . .

"The same evening, Roux's great-grandfather died of his snake-bite, and my grandfather and my father watched beside him, while I did not sleep from fright. And since then it has always been the same: we do not go up to Sauveplane except in time of trouble or, now and then, for festivals, such as the marriage of a daughter. . . .

"Moreover, at the change of the season, we always go by with the cart to see if the roof of our sheepfold still holds and to carry up a few straps. . . . At other times, when we go up to the mountain without the cart, we take short cuts, going straight up over Sauveplane through the midst of the beeches and over the meadows of Roquelongue. . . .

"All these stories bring me back to my story today: I went up, then, with the *gendarmes* as I had done at the time of the other misfortunes. On the road we talked about the war, and the police-sergeant, who knew a great deal, had a far from confident air. Eight hundred metres from the farm, at the last turn before you reach the fields, the police-sergeant said to me:

" 'Go on ahead, Finiels; the bird can't be in the nest; go and talk to those women a little. . . .'

"No doubt he was sorry for them and did not wish to upset them too much. I hastened my steps and reached the farm. The old woman was on her doorstep and the two sisters were working in the garden. I said to the old woman:

" 'Where is the boy?' "

" 'Do I know?'

" 'Perhaps not. But there may be others who do.'

" 'What others?'

" 'The government, perhaps.'

" 'Well, let them look, the boy is where he should be.' And not another word was to be got out of her.

"The two daughters went on with their work and were carrying greens to the rabbits. I thought to myself: 'They are hiding him; they know very well that he has not signed up.' And I felt myself losing my temper again.

"Roux's mother is a saintly woman, pious and upright, a hard worker and kind to the neighbours: she had taken care of my wife during an illness which she had got from a chill, but in my anger I was already forgetting these things. . . .

"All of a sudden up came my two *gendarmes*.

" 'Good evening, ladies and all the company,' said the sergeant politely.

" 'Good evening, gentlemen,' replied Finette (the name they gave to Roux's mother). 'Are you going up the mountain?'

" 'Not exactly; we are coming here for something. . . .'

"After a moment's silence the sergeant asked Finette:

" 'The boy isn't here?'

" 'Of course not. . . . He went off long ago.'

"Anger and also pity for these women went to my head. I felt that now I was embarrassing the *gendarmes* a little, so without saying good evening to anyone I took the road down and set out. The *gendarmes* remained behind to tell these women what they had to tell them. . . .

"I was going down then without haste when, about half way, the *gendarmes* overtook me. . . .

" 'The boy is not at Sauveplane,' the sergeant said to me, 'but he has not signed up either. He must have gone over into Spain, or perhaps . . .'

" 'Or perhaps?'

" '. . . he is hiding on the mountain. . . . In any case the women know where he is, but they will not say anything, and there is no way to make them. . . .'

" 'It is quite true perhaps that he is hiding on the mountain, for this is the good season. But in a month from now the nights will be sharp, and in two months it is quite likely to start snowing.'

" 'In two months the war will be over . . . but we shall certainly have caught our man.'

" 'Don't imagine it; the mountain is big and that boy knows it better than anybody. He may have difficulty finding anything to live on, but there will be no lack of hiding-places.'

" 'The best thing will be to watch the farm,' said the sergeant to the *gendarme,* while I repeated as I walked: 'What a monster, what a monster!'

"We arrived here: everybody already knew the news and the women had been repeating for an hour:

" 'Roux of Sauveplane has not signed up and the *gendarmes* are going to search for him.'

"Everybody was furious with Roux; they were saying:

" 'The Prussians might easily get to Montpellier, and even to Nîmes, if everybody acted like him.'

" 'They say that a great many of the rich have got out of it, but just the same the manager of the spinning-mill has enlisted.'

"Old Sanguinèdes—who died last year—was repeating to everybody:

" 'In 1870 the men had more courage. I almost went myself. I even got as far as Nîmes, and that was a different sort of war; it was a war in winter, and a bad winter.'

"People haven't any too much love for the *gendarmes* in our country, because of the wood and the fishing and hunting and the wagon lanterns, and a lot of other things as well, but just the same I made them come inside that day and take a glass of something strong. Almost all the men of the village came too, those at least who were not off to war. . . . There were Liron, Panard, Berthézène, and others who have died since."

In his corner, old Liron approved and remembered. Finiels continued:

"Then, after drinking, I said to the *gendarmes*:

" 'You might say this boy has done something that isn't good.'

" 'That's quite true,' added the others.

" 'He is a deserter,' said the *gendarme* who was new in the country and who looked at us as if we were animals.

"Seeing us all so well disposed, and myself particularly, the sergeant said to me:

" 'Finiels, that boy is not honest, he deserves to be sent to prison. . . . If he is hiding on the mountain, you will see him some day in the woods; then you will give us a sign, won't you?'

" 'That may very well be,' I answered, as I went back with him along the road. And on that we parted as good friends.

"We were all furious with Roux and I perhaps more than the others, because of my boy; but just the same the sergeant's question had done something to me. . . . *Gendarmes* are *gendarmes* and the rest of us work on the land; everyone has his own trade. Nevertheless, we were so angry with that boy that for once we might perhaps have helped the *gendarmes*. Panard kept repeating:

" 'If I meet him with my gun, I'll kill him like a wild beast.' "

"I was angry on account of my son-in-law who had gone to war, and because all our affairs were going to the dogs," broke in Panard, "but just the same I would perhaps have done him a bad turn just then."

"And I too," went on Finiels, "and all the men of the valley likewise. We had all agreed about this war: in our mountains no one had even thought of saying that we ought not to enlist, and we had let the young men of our families go without a moment's hesitation. You will understand, therefore, that we could not approve of a man who had not wished to do what all the others did. . . . But what made us still angrier perhaps was to know nothing certain in this affair."

" 'He is in Spain. He has been caught on the frontier,' some said to us, while others came and said: 'He is hiding on the mountain, behind Luzette, towards the forest of Oubrets. He comes down at night to Sauveplane to eat, and he never lets go of his rifle.'

"The guard of Luzette let it be understood that he was keeping his eyes open for him and he repeated ten times a day:

" 'I'll lead him to Saint-Jean by the ear.'

"But this was only gossip, and nobody knew anything certain

"The *gendarmes* however often prowled about Sauveplane, sometimes even in the middle of the night. . . . One morning, on my way to the station at dawn, I met them coming down from the mountain, as frozen as fishermen. But no news of Roux."

43

"MEANWHILE, the war was going on: winter drew near and the nights became long and cold. On the mountain there was already snow in spots, and the clouds came down over the upper pastures almost every day.

"If Roux was on the mountain, bad times were beginning for him, and we were well pleased, because for a long time misfortunes had begun to fall upon our families. Finiels of Vernède had been killed, Buffart of La Borie had had his leg cut off, there had been no more news from Randon the roadman for a good month. All these misfortunes had increased the anger of the countryfolk against Roux and even against his family. Finette and her two daughters remained shut up at Sauveplane: they no longer came down either to the market or to church. . . Just once the elder of the girls came to Saint-Jean to get some wool; they snubbed her perhaps twenty times in the shops, so much so that she went up again without buying anything. . . .

"Everybody was wrapped up in his own troubles. Finette and her daughters no longer left their farm, and, since nobody had anything new to tell about Roux, people were beginning to forget him a little when one day, just before the beginning of the severe winter, two women from the mountain who were carrying cheeses to Saint-Jean met him as they were coming down the short cuts of Roquelongue.

"This settled the matter. Roux was on the mountain, like a wild beast, like a mad dog that runs away from its master. It was natural to suppose that only fear could have driven him to this crazy deed, and this was no reason for us to excuse him. If he had been unwilling to go because his crops were not in or because he had to care for his beasts, and if he had stayed quietly at his farm, or, when things came to the worst, if he had received the *gendarmes* with rifle-shots, and if, in the end, he had hidden on the mountain to save his life, we would perhaps heve been able to understand him. I don't want to say that we should have thought he did right, but we should not have felt the same anger against him. But, in these first months of the war, we could not guess the reasons that had driven him to hide on the mountain, and on the face of things we could only despise him for having acted like a wild beast driven by fear, that does not know how to do anything useful either for others or for itself. . . .

"It was then that people began to call him 'Roux the Bandit.' You know, of course, that in the country you find 'Roux,' like 'Finiels,' on all the farms, at all the dairies, in all the villages. So, in order to avoid mistakes, you say 'Roux of Sauveplane,' 'Roux of Malet,' 'Roux of Vernède.' Consequently, we began to say 'Roux the Bandit' as before we had said 'Roux of Sauveplane.' We did not mean by this that he had murdered or stolen, but simply that he no longer belonged to any farm or village, and that he was something like a poacher on the mountain. . . .

"We felt sure that he must come down from time to time, in the middle of the night, to his mother's house, for a bite to eat and to lay in a few provisions. Without this manœuvre, he could not have lived a week on the mountain

45

where there was nothing to be found but wild bayberries and raspberries at the height of the warm weather. But we were sure that the watchfulness of the *gendarmes* and the neighbours must often prevent him from descending as far as Sauveplane and oblige him to get his daily dole of food on the mountain. And now that the winter had set in for good and cold would be added to hunger, we thought he was going to be punished for his folly and his evil action. During the first bad days of that year, this idea recurred to me every time I looked at the mountain. . . . Perhaps you don't know just what winter is like on the mountain?"

I flatter myself that I know the mountain well, almost as well as these men who know it profoundly. These words of Finiels vexed me and I contradicted them immediately, at the risk of interrupting the story he was telling me.

"But of course, Finiels . . . we have crossed the passes together in the bad season."

Finiels began to laugh.

"You have seen the snow and the storm, I remember: one real storm too, but in a safe place, with a good road under the snow, the village ahead, your head clear, a well-filled knapsack, and a draught of rum to set you up."

Finiels pronounced it "ron," but I knew quite well what he meant; I remembered this draught of rum taken in the storm, without which I should not perhaps have taken another step through the snow.

"Besides, even that was a safe part of the mountain, a part where you can get by. . . . If you wish to have a bad time, go off the road, turn to the right or the left into the forest or on the plateau: after a hundred yards you will no longer know where you are, and if you have ventured over the crests, you can call yourself a dead man."

Old Liron broke in:

"Before the road went through, no one crossed the mountain in wid-winter. At other times, people took the great trail over the crests, and even this was quite an undertaking. At the first notch there was a house, however, the only one at that time, which was called 'Campanette.' It took its name from a bell which the guard rang every hour through the bad days of autumn or when the winter was not too advanced and you might still expect travellers. . . . This did not prevent people from getting lost on the mountain, and sometimes they even circled for hours about the bell and died a hundred yards from the refuge without being able to find the door."

I had known these stories from my childhood. Campanette and its old guard and the score of tales that belong to them—the two *gendarmes* carried off by the storm, the Lozerotte family entirely buried by the snow, the merchant of Meyrueis eaten by wolves. . . . I felt I knew thoroughly the mountain that I had crossed many times in mid-winter and I rather suspected all those mountaineers of exaggerating the perils it offers.

These grave and restrained men—so different from the peasants of the neighbouring plain, who are often joyous and always excessive—do not know how to exaggerate or even change a story. Unlike the other Southerners, they do not know how to modify their moral world, their ideas and their feelings. They consider them always with the austere exactitude, the cold precision, of economical and provident men. When these mountaineers judge a man from the moral point of view, they never condemn utterly: even their custom of referring everything to the Bible has not been able to change them in this respect, and if, following Scripture, they speak of the wicked and the impious in every connection, it is only to express general condemnation; not to sit in judgment on anyone whom they know.

But, to make up, they always exaggerate the power of natural forces and, for them, the most trifling storm unhorns the cattle and the least flood carries away the whole valley. . . .

I knew too well this tendency of their minds not to be a bit sceptical when I heard them speak of the dangers of the mountain. These men, who are extremely mature morally, and who, through the wealth and richness of their emotions and their self-control, share in the most exacting civilisation, have none the less remained primitive in the presence of natural forces. . . .

The old mountaineer, sensing my distrust, persisted in trying to convince me:

"I remember those days of the Campanette: there were those terrible winters then when no word came down from the upper villages for two months. When people died, they carried them out into the snow, twenty yards from their houses, and did not bury them until spring. You found them weeks after, looking as if they had died there the evening before. . . .

"Now, the postman always goes as far as these villages, except during two or three bad weeks: so much so that you might think that the road had changed the climate of the mountain, and this is true for the inhabited parts and for the guard-houses.

"But as I told you just now, go a little to the right or the left off the road and you will find the old-time winter. I even found it once myself, fifteen years ago, and I can tell you about it. I had nimbler legs then than I have now, and stronger ones, yet I surely thought I had met my finish there. . . .

"This was before the war; Monsieur Rolland had come to the château for Christmas with a gentleman from Paris. It was a fine winter; beautiful weather, very dry and firm in the valley, which must mean frightful cold on the mountain.

"One fine day, monsieur came to find me, with this other gentleman from Paris.

" 'Finiels, we want to make an excursion to Aire de Côte.'

" 'There is a lot of snow up there, and we are getting near the time for bad weather. This is not the season for excursions, especially over by Aire de Côte, where there is no road. If you want to see wild country, monsieur would do better to come back this summer.'

" 'What we want is to see the wildest slope of the mountain covered with snow; we canot find a better guide than you. You must go with us. . . .'

49

"I protested. Monsieur had a thousand reasons for urging me and I ended by yielding.

"The next day, we set out at three o'clock in the morning; it was clear and very calm. We climbed up to Sauveplane, passed the little meadow, and found ourselves in the fir-grove: no snow yet . . . at three hundred metres from the gravel pit, we drew near the ubac fields, and all of a sudden, before we knew it, we were right in the snow, perhaps a yard and a half deep, already old and bearing us well.

"Day came, and we were on the peak and these gentlemen could see in all directions. . . . It was, as you say, picturesque: the morning fog lay deep over the valley and made a sort of sea just at the edge of the snow. Then, very far away, beyond this great sheet, we saw other mountains and other lands emerging.

" 'Finiels, what is that great plain, all white, on our left?'

" 'Montals lies behind you, giving you the direction of the low country. . . . It is not a plain, monsieur; quite the contrary, a high mountain: the Causse Méjean. It is almost as high as the mountains about here, but it is as flat as a floor for threshing wheat, with no more earth and as many stones.'

" 'So we have the sea at our backs; we should see it between the summits of the Basses-Cévennes. . . .'

" 'You can see it in fine, very dry weather, but today you cannot see anything but the ponds over by Cette and Montpellier. The same is true in all four quarters of the horizon.'

" 'What a wonderful observatory!' said Monsieur Rolland to that gentleman. 'It is truly one of the most significant spots in France. We have the Massif Central at our back, the valley of the Rhone at our left, and the Mediterranean in front of us. The point of solidity, the point of anarchical and brutal variations, and the point of harmonious variations. . . .'

"He said many other things which I cannot recall now and which perhaps I did not understand very well; but I listened to them with pleasure just the same, because I have always liked to hear capable men talk. When I have well understood a sentence, I remember it for ever, like that which I have just repeated to you.

"While they were talking, the sun had finally risen. . . . A true summer sun that made the little particles of snow dance, like grasshoppers in a meadow.

"The walking was easy; we had long slides under the beeches, and these gentlemen were enjoying the excursion. . . .

"We passed Campanette: you know there is nothing left now but the walls. The gentlemen made me tell them about it: the gentleman from Paris thought it was odd. He looked at the rampart from all sides:

" 'So you see, Rolland,' he said to monsieur, 'these fine monoliths and that handsome decoration: this is certainly no recent construction.'

"And they began asking me whether the old-timers had known Campanette, if any of them said they had seen it built.

ANDRÉ CHAMSON

"At last we ate a bite sitting in front of the door, and when we had finished I spoke about returning. But the gentlemen told me that they wanted to follow the old trail a little way, two or three kilometres, over towards the mountain.

" 'It is early,' monsieur told me. "They don't expect us before night.'

"So we took the trail and walked toward the mountain.... It was perhaps half-past eleven: the sun still fell full on the snow which hummed like a meadow. I could feel quite plainly that it was beginning to get too soft to hold us. At times it gave way and we sank in up to our knees or even to our thighs.

"The gentlemen followed the line of shade just under the fir-trees and there the snow still held well enough. . . . We passed the notch of Trescôumbos and climbed down a little way toward Bousuges. We were still following the trail when, all of a sudden, I found the forest right before our noses, and no trail, either to right or left. 'Wretch,' I said to myself, 'we have lost our way.' I turned round. I saw Montals on our left and far behind us. I told the gentlemen to bear to the right so as to find the trail again. They went in among the fir-trees: we walked ten minutes, no trail. At this spot the forest was old and the snow bore us well because of the shade. All at once we stumbled on a younger growth; the snow no longer held, and there we were in the drifts up to our hips, still looking for that trail on our right.

"The gentlemen, who walked well for gentlemen from the city, began to give out and I myself thought, each time,

52

It was beginning to get too soft to hold us.

that I could not budge from my hole in the snow. I kept saying:

" 'The trail is twenty yards to the right; we will find snow that will bear us, further down the slope.'

"But after twenty yards there was no more trail than before, only other still deeper drifts.

"Then Monsieur Rolland began to say:

" 'You are mad, Finiels: we shall never get out. You are too far to the right, come back on the left. We shall find snow that will carry us.'

"I turned again and still saw Montals on the left and behind: we didn't want to get on to the plain to lose our way in the fir-groves. I said to monsieur:

" 'I don't want to contradict you, but I am going to the right. We shall get to the valley finally. Go to the left if you like, but you are a dead man.'

"Night came on: mild, but so black that you could not see three steps ahead. This was just our luck; the snow was not going to freeze until the small hours, perhaps it was even going to stay soft all night. . . .

"We still bore to the right, without finding the trail; fatigue gripped us and we had nothing left to eat. The gentleman from Paris slid into the snow-holes like a dead man falling into his grave: every few minutes we had to stop to let him get back his strength. . . . We spent the night circling like this, in the snow, like mad dogs. . . .

"In the morning, the cold hardened the snow and we were able to walk with less difficulty. But I did not recognise the mountain any longer and turned in all directions without finding a trail; I still bore to the right, like a madman, without even knowing why I did so. . . . The day dawned still warm and I felt that the snow was going to melt again. . . .

"To be brief, we wandered all day on the plateau, and it was only at five o'clock in the evening, that we stumbled upon Borie de Côte, like famished wolves, dead with fatigue. . . ."

Old Liron broke in:

"And the son of the guard of Cap de Coste who was found dead last year in the storm, fifty yards from his home. . . .

"Yet he was a steady, capable fellow, who was quite at home on the mountain. He had taken the field with the infantry and always in the worst spots. He had married since the war and stayed on at Saint-Jean; he worked in the spinning-mill and earned a good living, especially toward the end.

"Last Christmas, he got the idea of going to visit his father on the mountain. He set out on a very calm day, and his wife stayed at Saint-Jean and never thought of worrying for a moment.

"It was fair all day in the valley, but in the evening a storm broke over the mountain.

"You know that the guard's house, on the Cap de Coste, is not precisely on the worst part of the mountain. It is almost on the road, and on the side that is best sheltered from the wind from above. But on this day it was just over these parts that the storm broke.

"The wind glided over the snow and detached fragments of ice that spun over it like the stones that children skip over water: and this snow and this ice whirled all night like a foaming torrent.

"The guard, who did not know that his boy was on the way up, closed his double door and went to bed quite calmly.

"Nobody knows what this boy went through that night about the house where his father slept.

"The next day the storm slackened and the old man took advantage of this to go and see whether many trees had been blown down. This was his whole duty: he watched the trees, in winter because of storms and in summer because of fire. . . .

"You know that fifty metres before you reach the refuge the road passes over a little bridge: the storm had driven the snow to one side, and on the other the ground was clear. Crossing the bridge, the old man saw a soldier's knapsack partly buried in the snow. He climbed down to pick it up, and there, under the bridge that made a sort of grotto or shepherd's hut in the snow, he found his son, seated, his eyes open straight before him, his fingers in his mouth, stiff in death, killed by the cold. . . ."

"This is to show you," Finiels went on, "that you can't fool with the mountain in winter. . . .

"This is why all the countryside thought that Roux would end by giving himself up.

" 'He'll come down, like the wild boars, before the snow,' they said. But plenty of snow had fallen, and Roux the Bandit had not come down from the mountain.

"The *gendarmes* were still watching the slopes of Sauveplane, but they never caught sight of our man. Once, however, they met him at nightfall and almost caught him: they fired several shots at him at long range and too hastily. . . .

"I was working that day in my vineyard at the end of the slope, over by the four roads. It is our vineyard farthest up on the mountain, the highest in the whole country. There are a few old-time terraces, a little sandy earth, and good flints to make a fire: we make a wine up there that is not first-class perhaps but I'm used to it and like it. Then, too, it's very little trouble, and we have so few vineyards over here that we must take good care of those that we have. . . .

"Well, I was in this good sunny corner, busy pruning, when I caught sight of the *gendarmes* passing on the road, three hundred metres above my vineyard. It was all of half-past four to five o'clock and toward the end of the winter: night was beginning to fall and the fog rose from the valley. The two 'blues' were walking slowly toward Sauveplane, and I thought they were going to watch the approaches to it, always for the same reason. . . . I was not surprised: this was not the first time I had seen them at this trick. You see they must have had orders from the town: we should have been quite glad to see them catch Roux the Bandit, because his story set tongues wagging and because he was a bad example even for those who appeared to be most angry with him. . . .

"So I finished pruning the vines as long as it was light enough to see: then I thrust my bundle into the hut which we have at the bottom of the vineyard and prepared to go down. As I was coming down my terraces I heard a gun-shot over toward Sauveplane—not the sound of a hunter's gun but the sharp crack of an army rifle. I had forgotten my *gendarmes* and I stopped, saying to myself:

" 'Who is out after wild boars at this hour?'

"I turned toward Sauveplane and then in a few seconds, three other rifle-shots began to crackle like hail among the fields of ubac.

" 'The devil,' I said to myself, 'this is a fusillade.' And all of a sudden I remembered my *gendarmes* and added: 'You don't know how truly you spoke! They must have surprised Roux near the farm and they are doing for him.'

"I was eager to go and see what was happening, but I was afraid of finding the boy stretched out dead by his farm, or wounded to death by the *gendarmes* and dying before his mother's eyes. I would not have known just how to behave because of Finette and her girls; so I returned here quietly, almost certain that Roux had been killed by the *gendarmes*.

"Here everybody was already talking of the thing, as they usually do. They had seen the *gendarmes* passing, they had heard the rifle-shots, and this was enough to make them believe that Roux the Bandit had been killed on his way to his farm.

"We should have liked to be sure of this at once, but we were all held back by the fear of finding ourselves with those women before the body of the boy. Although we had been angry with him, when we thought perhaps he had just died like a soldier in the war we felt a sort of pity for him.

"We expected to see the *gendarmes* appear every minute, and toward nine o'clock they did actually arrive, just as we were beginning to close our doors. But they tried to pass without saying anything and to go straight through to Saint-Jean. Liron, who recognised them, stopped them and asked:

" 'So there's been hunting on the mountain today?'

" 'It's not the season,' replied the sergeant. 'Hunting is not permitted.'

" 'There are some who can hunt without permission.'

"But the *gendarmes* walked on and did not appear to wish to talk. I had overheard Liron, from my doorstep, so I came up myself and asked them:

" 'You haven't seen anyone on the mountain?'

" 'Nobody today,' the sergeant answered as he moved away.

" 'They have missed their man,' Liron said to me, and at that we went to bed.

"This was true. Later we learned the details of the affair, but from the first day we understood how it had happened. . . . As the *gendarmes* were on watch near the farm, they had seen Roux come out upon the little meadow near the fir-grove. The sergeant must have lost his head a bit and he had shouted to Roux to give himself up, when he was still a hundred metres away from them and close to the edge of the forest. Roux had made for the woods and the *gendarmes* had fired at him four times without being able to take good aim, because of the night and his running. Once Roux had disappeared into the forest, they

59

Roux had made for the woods.

had not wished to pursue him over the mountain, in the middle of the night. This would have been quite useless anyhow, since they did not know the short-cuts and the passes of the neighbourhood. So they had climbed down, none too proud of themselves and unwilling to speak to anybody about the matter.

"That year we had bad weather on our mountains toward the end of winter. A snow-storm gripped the country for a whole week. It came from Roccalte and fell on Luzette for a whole day, and the following day Luzette seemed to send it back to Roccalte.

"After this snow, the storm came up from the direction of Rouergue and we had rain for a fortnight. This was not, as in autumn, a heavy rain, that swelled the mountain brooks into torrents and brought disaster to the valley. It was a little steady rain. with sometimes a good hour of sunlight during the day. . . . You know that sort of weather. It is good for making consumptives, and when it invades the country nobody can keep warm, because the dampness is everywhere (in the sheets on the beds as on the walls of the bedrooms, on the stones of the chimney as on those of the doorstep). When it snows, the air is clear and you can manage to get warm, but with this fine rain you shiver all day long. . . . It was indeed bad weather for Roux in his hiding-places on the mountain, where the rain must have soaked in as into the bed of the river.

"But after this snow and rain, the winter was over. We no longer heard anything of Roux and we thought some misfortune had befallen him during this end of the bad season. People were saying:

" 'It will have done him no good not to do as the others. He must have perished on the mountain, while he might perhaps have come back from the war.'

"At the beginning of that spring, I had to pass through Sauveplane, according to my wont, with the cart.

"I have already told you that after the bad winter season, when the roads became firm, we went up on the mountain to look after our sheepfold. The winter weather never did the building any good: it tore away the tiles, it rotted the beams, it loosened the big nails of the doors better than a pair of pincers could, and it crumbled the strongest cement into sand like that from the river. So we had to take along a few tools to repair the roof, the doors, and the barriers of the sheepfold. We also had to take along the iron bed, our herdsman's straw mattress and cooking utensils, because, if we left them up there during the winter, we could not keep them. Every time we found our mattress rotted and our pots eaten away with rust.

"For all this luggage we had to take the cart, and with the cart we were forced to pass through Sauveplane. . . .

"So that year, as on others, I passed before Finette's door, starting off on my trip up the mountain. I had not seen it since the day when I came there with the two *gendarmes,* and I must say I was far from calm at the idea of finding myself before it.

"I wondered if I had better pass without speaking, averting my face from her door, or if it was better to stop and pay her a brief visit, as I had been accustomed to do for twenty years.

"Because of my anger against her son, I should have liked to pass without speaking, but on the other hand I had reasons for pitying her and even esteeming her. After all, she was like the rest of us, deprived of her boy and all alone with her two daughters, on the rough land, with work too heavy for women. . . .

"Nevertheless, up to the last moment, I did not quite know what I was going to do, and I was still of two minds as I followed the road that climbs up to Sauveplane. But when I had turned the corner before the spring, beside the three poplars, and found myself before the farm, I stopped my horse as I was wont to do, without hesitating.

"Everything was in order and nothing had changed, apart from the rye-fields that had not been tilled. La Finette was at her door and looked at me without stirring. She was not going to be the first to speak and she was quite right.

"I called out to her and jumped down from my cart; she came toward me and we began to talk in the usual way. We talked about the soil and the beasts, then about the winter which was quite likely to have harmed the sheepfolds on the mountain, and finally about the fine weather which did not yet seem entirely settled, and which might let the Rouergue come back over the valley.

"In all this talk there was not a word about her son, in spite of my desire to know what had happened during these last weeks. I wondered if she knew her boy was safe in some hiding-place, or if, on the contrary, she pictured him dead in some lonely spot on the mountain, and I looked at her askance to try and divine what was in her head.

"She looked tired and was certainly sad, but, as she had always had this air of sadness, one could not attach any significance to it and this languor was indeed a part of her very nature.

"I had to go away without learning anything, but this visit to La Finette had taught me something just the same, and that day, as I was following the great trail, I told myself over and over that this war, no matter how one took it, brought misfortune to everybody."

I I I

"About this time the son of Pagès, who had been in the war from the beginning, came home to spend a leave of convalescence; he had been hit in the shoulder, which did not prevent him from going about and looking after his affairs.

"As the snow had completely disappeared from the peaks, he took it into his head to go and see if the roof of his sheepfold, at Pueylong, had suffered much from the bad weather. . . . This sheepfold is in one of the worst spots on the mountain, far beyond ours, in the direction of Aire de Côte. The snow lasts there for more than six months, but in summer there is good grass for the beasts and there is always shade along its borders and running water at the foot of its meadows.

"Pagès, then, took the short-cuts up Aire de Côte, passed the meadow of Roquelongue, and began to follow the ridge.

"He had not gone five hundred metres under the beeches (at least this is how he told me the story himself) when he saw a man coming toward him. A man still young, with his clothes in tatters, a long beard, and streaming hair.

"When this man was only a few steps away he stopped directly in front of Pagès, calling him by name.

"Pagès recognised Roux and thought at first that it was a *trève** he had before him. But it was actually Roux the Bandit who was speaking to him, as much alive as you or I.

---

* That is, the conventional ghost.

"Pagès felt a rush of anger, and, in spite of his wounded shoulder, he wanted to leap on Roux and drag him off to Saint-Jean by the collar of his jacket. He would not have had much difficulty in doing so, for Roux was a mere shadow of himself, after his winter hardships.

"As they stood face to face, Pagès gave way to his anger and asked Roux, 'Why didn't you do like the rest of us?'

"He did not ask him this question with any idea of listening to his reply, but simply shouted his anger at him, so that for a few minutes Roux was prevented from saying a word, while Pagès kept saying to him:

" 'Finiels of Vernède was killed four months ago; Randon has been listed as missing since September. My shoulder is smashed and Buffart from Borie has lost a leg. You, all this time, have stayed here, quite at your ease.'

"But Roux, by dint of obstinacy and patience, succeeded just the same in making himself heard. Calmly, gravely, he set himself to explain his conduct, and Pagès, who had thought like all of us that he had been afraid to enlist, was astonished to hear him give good reasons for not doing so.

"To tell the truth, Pagès has never been able to repeat to us all that Roux managed to say to him that day, but the evening after this meeting he replied unceasingly to all the questions put to him:

" 'He is not a bad man. He did not wish to do what he had to do, but you can't say that he is not doing right. . . . He is a man of God, who could not go off like the rest of us because he understands things that we do not understand.'

"We had a fine dispute with Pagès that evening, all of us old people of the village. If he had not just come back from the war, and wounded as well, we should have howled him down like some urchin who doesn't know what he is talking about.

"Old Pagès shouted to his boy, 'If you think he has done well you have only to do the same thing, you rapscallion.'

"But Pagès replied, 'Everybody does as he thinks right. I have my reasons for going to war, but Roux has his for not wishing to enlist.'

" 'Fine reasons,' his father answered him, 'reasons of a rapscallion.'

" 'Reasons that are understandable,' Pagès continued. But when we asked him to explain them to us, he did not know what to say.

" 'He talked to me for an hour better than a pastor; the good God seemed to be speaking from his mouth and everything he said about himself was like passages from Scripture. He repeated to me over and over: "The Eternal has abandoned the world, and the world is mad. You do well to act as you do, and in the madness of the world your submission is wisdom. But we do not need to be deaf to the Eternal or to despise His word, and it is to follow His teachings and to keep His law that I have refused to go to war." '

"All these explanations only increased our anger, and old Pagès spoke for us when he answered his son:

" 'If he has something to say to the good God, he should share the suffering of the others, instead of refusing to submit to it.'

"But Pagès persisted in defending Roux, and he retorted to his father:

" 'He suffers as much as the rest of us, and I would not change my troubles for his. He has more to complain of than many people who pretend they have gone to war, but who have never been in the bad places, and have done nothing but parade around in automobiles.'

" 'He has bewitched you with all his reasons, but you should understand that he cannot be as badly off as he has made you believe: he must have found out how to get food somehow, on the mountain.'

" 'He can't get much of anything to have become so thin, even if he comes down from time to time to see his mother. . . . But it is not hunger or storms that bring him his greatest sufferings: if he is to be pitied it is for having to stay always in the wilderness, never having anybody to talk to, and spending his time like an animal, hiding from men. . . . If he had not been at school with me, he would have fled at the sight of me, as he always does when he meets anyone on his path: but we were always good comrades before the war, we spent a whole summer together cutting wood on the summit of Luzette, and besides, our families are somewhat related: it is because of all this that he couldn't help coming to talk to me a little, and I don't regret having kept him company for an hour.'

"As Pagès warmed up more and more in this dispute, we finally all wearied of contradicting a man who had come back from the war, and who had more right to talk than any of us. Old Pagès himself could only reply to his boy:

"I know very well that Roux was not a bad friend before he committed that folly. I have always said he was one of the most honest men in the valley, and I was well pleased when I saw you take a job with him. . . . But since that time, he has done something that should not be done, and you have no right to let him off so easily.'

" 'Everybody does as he believes,' resumed Pagès, 'and Roux has his reasons for not wanting to fight.'

"Although I wasn't on Pagès side, I was not as angry as the others and I followed the dispute especially to try to form some idea about this affair. What seemed to me most blameworthy in Roux's conduct was his having condemned himself to live without doing anything useful. I said to myself:

" 'What does he ever do with himself in the forests, on the mountain? He can only spend his time in idleness while his valley lands waste away like other people's, as they would have wasted away if he had gone to war.'

"To be assured about this thing, I asked Pagès if he could tell me how Roux spent his days on the mountain, and Pagès replied:

" 'I asked him that, and he said, "I walk and I pray, I have a Bible, and I read it under the beeches, then I go and stretch out on the rocks on the summit, and I look at the valley and the villages.

" ' "When it is cold, I sleep by day in the sun, between two rocks that protect me from the wind, and I spend my nights walking on the mountain, along the deserted trails.

" ' "Even during the worst weather, it is difficult for me to light a fire when the wind is blowing hard, because the smoke would soon betray me. But I light it sometimes in the caves and remain for hours before the burning logs, then before the red embers, as if I were back in the winter evenings at Sauveplane." ' "

Finiels stopped speaking for a few minutes: we respected this silence, but our suspended attention did not allow it to become an interruption of the story. . . . The dogs outside were bewailing their fatigue from the hunt and their regret for the morning's run. Their plaintive baying—as if in chase—brought before us the night's excursion, the long walk on the mountain, following the trail over the fine, close-cropped grass, the waiting for the frosty dawn at the highest corner of the beech wood: this waiting, which had been, for me, not a vigil, but only an attentive reverie, induced by the sight of the three slopes of this great promontory, that fall perpendicularly toward the triple valley and the high meadows of the land about Sauveplane. . . .

But old Finiels took up his tale again, and it was to me that he addressed himself directly, as if he had to convince me, as if it were necessary for him to prove something to me.

"You know, Monsieur André, I am no great habitué of the chapel. You see, it is a long time since I have gone there, except for marriages and baptisms, for the sake of propriety. . . . But you know too that I respect the faith of others and that I even admire those who put the word of God into practice."

This was not the first time that Finiels had tried to assure me of his detachment and of his respect for religious things. Many a time, during our excursions on the mountain, when we were walking side by side and the going was not too hard, he had acquainted me with the grounds for his doubts. I have discussed them with him, adopting his point of view, using the language and the images familiar to him. In these discussions, we have always been in complete accord regarding such problems, and since Finiels had gathered from this that I believed him to be an atheist, and considered him free from all the bonds of religion, he has taken pains very frequently to assure me of his respect for religious matters, perhaps through a taste for moderation, and, no doubt, also through an instinct for his veritable affinities. But these declarations were quite useless and I could not be the dupe of our dialogues: when I examined them in solitude, far from concluding that Finiels was indifferent, I associated him, on the contrary, with that religious and almost ascetic race to which he belonged.

Finiels had not been able to remain Protestant, as his fathers had not been able to remain Catholic; but these ruptures with the Church were still religious acts. This tendency to heresy, this taste for theological controversies and for the schisms which they arouse, is only the result of a mystical application of the soul. Heresies, even negations, cannot give the right to pretend to indifference in regard to religious things; they prove, on the contrary, that the examination of religion is, to the spirit, the only research that matters.

In behaving in this way, Finiels was only obeying the genius of his race. Since the tenth century, simple pastors have prophesied on the mountains of the three Gardons and of Hérault, and the annals of the great abbeys of the Cévennes, that bear witness to their presence, all prove them to have had a miraculous eloquence and something like a mystical possession of the Word. I have often regretted that their improvisations have never been transcribed and that it is not even possible for us to find their primitive themes in the oral traditions and the proverbs of the mountain. At least we can imagine their tendencies from the more recent religious crises that have convulsed this region.

These mountaineers did not desire a learned and measured initiation, but a sudden and complete revelation. It was no doubt for this reason that they turned away from Albigensianism, a doctrine more subtle than mystical, more rhetorical than eloquent, and that a few centuries later they adopted the Reformation with enthusiasm.

The New Religion exalted their tendency to lyricism and their taste for prophecies. With the Old Testament and the Apocalypse it delivered to them unreservedly the inexhaustible themes that Catholicism had indeed presented to them, but with too much prudence—perhaps too much moderation—for their taste, and in a fashion that was more material than verbal.

Today, the majority of these men seek to free themselves from the practices of Protestantism, but if they do not wish to go to church, as their ancestors did not wish any longer to go to mass, for all that, they do not lose their respect for sacred things, and it is still religious discussions that delight them most. They pretend to be indifferent, but when they converse gravely, the only problems they can bring up are those of sin, death, and eternal life. . . .

Having allowed a few seconds of silence to elapse after his profession of faith, Finiels went on:

"When I knew that Roux the Bandit had not yielded to fear, but to his conscience, and that he had not wished to go and fight because the Scripture said, 'Thou shalt not kill,' I felt less angry with him.

"I did not think he was right, and I would not have told others to act like him, but I respected his belief. Everything he had said to Pagès caused me to reflect, and I could no longer think of him as an animal you hunt, but rather as a capable man with whom you talk things over.

"But work and the anxieties of war and of my property obliged me to think of many other things. Time passed: hard times for everybody. Now and then, the boy left us without news for a week or two, which caused us as much anguish as if he had been killed. All the plots of land which I had, here and there, had to be tilled, and, with only my two hands, I never got to the end of my work.

"During this time, Roux was still on the mountain. He became a little less wary and at rare intervals someone from this neighbourhood would meet him going to cut his wood over by Roquelongue. He only approached those whom he knew well or who were in some way related to him on one side or the other, and all these people came back saying the same thing as Pagès—so much so that a few old people were already reporting that the Holy Ghost spoke through Roux's mouth. . . .

"I have already told you that Roux, before his act of desperation, was not a great talker, and that he lived a rather shut-in life, but I must also tell you that when he spoke, he spoke well, especially when he wanted to explain something. If he took a fancy to make a speech, he brought out for you phrases and words that seemed to come from another tongue, but that astonished you without giving you any desire to laugh.

"He spoke in patois, like the rest of us, because it is the most convenient language and because we are used to it, but he spoke French perhaps as well as you do and not like us who get the words wrong half the time."

Old Finiels gave me a laughing, sidelong glance:

"You speak patois very well, Monsieur André, but you would have to go a long way to speak it as well as Roux spoke French."

All the listeners began to laugh. These mountaineers could not understand the pleasure I took in talking to them in patois. If they admired me a little because I spoke their language almost as well as they did, they never missed a chance to point out to me the mistakes that slipped into some of my phrases.

This was a very friendly malice, and perhaps it was also, unconsciously, a way of getting even, the search for a basis of equality between them and myself.

Though they knew that I was of their race, through birth and through many years of a mountaineer's life, these men felt that I was different because, as they said, "I had studied in many cities." I am no longer a peasant, like my grandfathers whom they knew, and in their minds this difference raised me above them. It would have deprived them of all confidence in me if I had not shown them some weakness, and this weakness they found in my taste for their tongue, in my little errors of syntax or semantics. These little errors—which they corrected with a smile—compensated in their eyes for the superiority which my studies gave me; they permitted us to meet on an equal footing like people of the same origin who, when everything is said and done, are all equals and all limited by the same weaknesses and the same uncertainties.

It is for this reason that I have been able to retain all their confidence, as if I were a peasant of their valley, a mountaineer of their mountain; and this reason, far from seeming to me paltry or disproportioned to its results, seems to me, on the contrary, marvellously symbolic and quite as noble as their confidence itself.

The errors which they observed in my patois phrases were not, in fact, simple material errors, a lack of experience and mechanical training: they were, on the contrary, the mark of my difference and a sort of confession of my acquired weaknesses; they came from a literary knowledge of their language, a veritable modification of the spirit. And they were quite right to see in them nothing but errors, childish errors which it is right to reprove and correct, even when they have a learned origin and are justified by the dictionaries and the manuals of philology.

But they know I am grateful, none the less, for this knowledge of their language. It has brought me their daily confidence and just now this story of Roux which they would probably not have related thus to anybody who did not belong to their race, who could not answer them in the speech of Sauveplane, Saint-Jean, and Bessède.

It is even surprising that Finiels did not tell me this story in patois, as he had already told me many others, thus imposing the *langue d'oc* on all his listeners and on myself.

Only a subtle chance had determined today the choice of the French language, and I believe I have found the cause in the slightly emphatic character of the first phrases of my old friend. The almost solemn declaration with which he began the story of Roux could only have been made by him in French, as when a witness in court he could use only the French tongue to take oath and give his testimony. . . . When the laughter was over and the few *raïoles*· rejoinders unloosed by this buffoonery had died down with the laughter, Finiels resumed the thread of his story, thus putting an end to my reflections.

· *"Raïou, -ole.* Sobriquet of the inhabitants of the Cévennes, especially the mountain folk who inhabit the Southern valleys and slopes of Lozère."—Mistral, *Lou Tresor dou Felibrige.*

"So there was nothing miraculous in the fact that this boy spoke well, since he could do so before his act of folly, whenever he wished. But all the same, what we heard of the talks which he gave on the mountain appeared to us very extraordinary, and we wondered if this manner of speaking was not a sign. . . . A man who talks well is always possessed by something, by something greater than himself: the avaricious and the egotistical never succeed in speaking well and their language becomes confused whenever they try to say anything. Thus the speeches of Roux, reported by those who had met him in some spot on the mountain, made everyone reflect, and this became still worse on the day when Deleuze, after having met him on the mountain, began to defend him, in his turn.

"You know Deleuze: he is a man who is as much listened to in the country by believers, whether Huguenots or Catholics, as he is by those who do not attend either church. And this is only right, for he knows how to tell the truth about everything, and because in sixty years he has not made a single enemy in the valley. Besides, he is a man of property who is both thrifty himself, and at the same time gives to those who are in need through no fault of their own. All these things Deleuze does because he is a believer and because he wishes to put the Scripture into practice, and I can tell you that if all those who belong to the chapel resembled him a little, even remotely, they would see me no doubt more often at service, and I should not be the only one to go. . . .

"Well, towards the end of the fine days of 1915, Deleuze, who had gone up on the mountain for mushrooms, met Roux in a deserted part of the plain of Montals.

"They had a long talk about religion and the times and Deleuze could find no fault with anything Roux the Bandit said. On the contrary he was amazed by the way in which this boy justified his words and his acts. When he tried to say something or explain himself, he uttered first a few phrases of his own, then he quoted passages from Scripture that said the same thing.

"Deleuze has spoken to us often about this meeting because, curious as we were to know the details of it, we gave him a good opportunity to make us listen to the word of God. . . . He has even set a marker in my wife's Bible at a few of the passages which Roux had quoted to him that day. I am going to find them again, and I think I still remember the way in which they are arranged."

Finiels rose and took up the heavy black Bible which his wife had placed in the chimney corner, behind the salt-box decorated with lozenges and the multi-coloured calendar of the Maison Nisolle. . . . It was the big common Bible which the peddlers of 1830 had left in all the houses on the mountain, *The Holy Bible, or the Old and the New Testament—stereotyped edition from the version revised by J. F. Ostervald, published by the Protestant Biblical Society of Paris, 1823.*" On every page, two long columns of crowded fine type held your attention forcibly, fixed it upon a verse until, weary of the monotony of the page and the characters, it freed itself from the bondage of the printed text and remained solitary, in a kind of dream, with the verse already read.

Finiels turned over the leaves of this Bible, looking for the little markers that were placed between the pages. When he found a marker, he kept the page with a finger and began to read a few passages to himself, going from one to another, as if to find the proper sequence and the key to a complex construction.

Then, like a child with a school-book, following the lines with his finger and no longer moving either his hand or his body, Finiels set himself to give a meaning to all these passages:

"When Deleuze began to reproach Roux for his behaviour, without accusing him of anything definite, could the boy have answered better than by this phrase from the Psalms: 'Who can understand his errors? Cleanse thou me from secret faults.' But when Deleuze began to reproach him for not having been willing to enlist, Roux the Bandit had no difficulty in showing him that the Scripture forbade making war. I do not read you these passages, because everybody knows them and nobody disputes them. Certainly, Deleuze would have been the last to do so, and he agreed at once with Roux on this point. But he told him that it was not for him to set this example when wiser men than he submitted to the laws of the world. Listen now to the reply which the Scriptures offered Roux, and tell me if one could speak with more wisdom: 'The law of the Lord is perfect, converting the soul: the testimony of the Lord is sure, making wise the simple.' How many other passages of the Scriptures seem made on purpose for Roux; first to express his misery, like this:

" 'I was a reproach among all mine enemies, but especially among my neighbours, and a fear to mine acquaintance: they that did see me without, fled from me, I am forgotten as a dead man out of mind; I am like a broken vessel.' Then how could you find better words than these to affirm his confidence: 'Lord, Thou hast been our dwelling-place in all generations. Before the mountains were brought forth or ever Thou hadst formed the earth and the world, even from everlasting to everlasting, Thou art God.' And do you not think that there is a sort of promise that applies especially to the story of Roux in this other passage:

" 'I will lift up mine eyes unto the hills from whence cometh my help. My help cometh from the Lord, which made heaven and earth.'

"You see, there are plenty of good reasons in these passages, and I don't need to go on to make you realize that, talking in this way, Roux and Deleuze fell into agreement about many things. They agreed so well that when Deleuze got up to go because night was coming on, Roux asked him to say a prayer with him, before leaving him alone on the mountain.

"You know, it is a custom of those who attend church to say their prayers out loud, in each other's presence, in order to strengthen and give themselves courage. For my part, I believe this is a good custom: and we all make use of it more or less when we tell each other our troubles. I even believe that I am doing about the same thing when I am ploughing a bit of bad land with old Bloun and I talk to him all the time to encourage him to pull hard. . . .

"So Deleuze and Roux the Bandit prayed together in this lonely nook of the mountain. It is a lost spot, behind Montals, in the midst of the beech trees, in a valley full of springs and little streams. Under the beeches, there are heavy swards, more than a hundred years old perhaps and dotted with mushrooms after the autumn rains.

"Deleuze, who had placed his basket on the grass, fell on his knees under a tree: Roux did the same and Deleuze made his prayer. When he had finished, Roux the Bandit began to pray in his turn, and in such a manner that Deleuze believed he felt a benediction pass with each of his words. . . .

"When the prayer was finished, Roux and Deleuze rose, facing each other, in the heavy darkness that was falling on the mountain. Deleuze has repeatedly told us that at this moment he felt Roux firm in his belief and filled with the certitude that he should persevere in the same way, in that way which he had chosen from a clear and definite belief and not fleeing like an animal driven by fear. . . .

"But the night was coming on. Deleuze had a good two hours' walk to make before he reached his farm, and this through the steep short cuts which are hard going after dark. Just as he was leaving, Deleuze wished to let Roux know that he did not condemn his conduct in itself, but that he thought it useless:

" 'It would have been necessary for all the men in the world to climb up together on the mountains of their own countryside when they were told to go and fight; then perhaps the Lord would have come and sat in the midst of them. . . . But you are all alone on your mountain. . . .'

"But as Deleuze was going, Roux shouted to him through the darkness this phrase from the Psalms:

" 'There shall be an armful of corn in the earth upon the top of the mountain; the fruit thereof shall shake like Lebanon: and they of the city shall flourish like grass of the earth.'

"Upon these words, Deleuze left Roux the Bandit on the mountain, and as though it had happened purposely the wind rose that moment, the first wind of winter that brought the bad weather over our country.

"All that winter, we heard no more talk of Roux: in the bad weather no one goes up the mountain, and we ourselves never went toward Sauveplane, but always over by the valley. Besides, Roux could not have stayed at his mother's, for, four or five times, the *gendarmes* came down there without warning, in the morning, and they never found anybody there. So the boy must have stayed on the mountain, in the midst of the snow, as he had done the preceding year.

"People said that he lived on the very top of Luzette, in a grotto that overlooked the slope of Borie. The thing was quite possible, but it would not prevent him from suffering from the storms or from risking his life in the snow as he went out to get food. They say, however, that he had arranged things like a watch-tower, raising a wall of sharp stones before his cave."

"And that is no lie," Panard asserted. "I saw this hiding-place—this watch-tower, if you prefer—some time after Roux had left the mountain. It was still quite new and did not look deserted.

"We came near passing it without seeing it, but the shepherd of Randon, who was with us, pointed it out to us. He said to us:

" 'There is Roux's second house.'

"And when we said he was crazy, he answered:

" 'I know what I am saying, and I don't need to say how I know it. Come and see.'

"It was on the highest slope of Luzette. We climbed up through that little meadow which separates the last rampart of the crest from the great rocks that fall sheer above Borie. At the end of this meadow, there is a spring, and below the rampart there are two or three caves. Before the largest, Roux had raised a wall. At the foot of this wall he had placed a bench, and from this spot he could see the whole valley. . . . From these heights, you followed the windings of the road and the curves of the paths, as if it were a picture and, except at night or through the fog, no one could have approached without being observed two hours in advance.

"It seemed that Roux had cut some inscriptions on the flat stones of his cave. Those who were with us had read all sorts of stories there, and some words. . . ."

"What words?"

"I can't tell you. I don't read much and I couldn't bother to read what he wrote there on the stones, for that is always most difficult. . . . But it must have been inscriptions of God's Word, some passages from Scripture or bits of hymns. . . .

"Well, this wall stopped up half the cave. On the left hand, on the side that was still open, there was a row of utensils that Roux had manufactured. There were several kinds of stone mortars, such as you still find on farms. He must have used them for making meal from the ears of rye which he gathered in abandoned fields on the mountain, and I think he must have baked his bread there in the worst of the bad weather, for on one side, in a hole in the cliff, he had a sort of oven arched over with flat stones. . . .

"On the other side, over by the wall of loose stones, you saw a sort of bed of fir branches, arranged between this wall and the side of the cave; a few tufts of grass and mosses made the pillow, and it was as well arranged as was possible for a solitary man who has only his hands, stones from the mountains, and branches from the forest. . . ."

"That wouldn't help much," Finiels resumed, "a wall of dry stones, fir needles, and the vault of a cave would not count for much in this country where the houses are no good for winter unless they have walls a yard and a half thick and well-joined double doors. . . . It must have been the earth that kept him warmest, and the snow also, for they always have a kind of natural softness and never bite like water or stone. . . . You can imagine this existence: the privations and the loneliness of this boy always at prayer in the midst of the snow.

"This new winter was as rough as the last; if the snow came a little later on the mountain, it stayed there longer and the storms were perhaps more severe than the year before. When we heard no more talk of Roux and saw this bad weather cover the vineyards, we began to think again that he was dead.

"People said: 'He must have been eaten by wild beasts, we shall find nothing but his bones after the snow is gone.'"

"Eaten by wild beasts." I smiled as I heard Finiels use this formula.

I know that in his mind, as in that of all the peasants of these mountains, this phrase evoked the idea of a mysterious world. I found in it that creative tendency of the cosmogonal and zoological fables and legends, that instinctive exaggeration of all natural forces.

These mountaineers believe seriously in the existence of a whole redoubtable fauna, a terrible and monstrous bestiary. This is not from ignorance of the animals that really live in their forests. On the contrary, they know these intimately and they have even amassed precise observations about each one, that show them to be a race of predestined naturalists.

But alongside of this almost scientific knowledge, they leave room for fabulous fancies: the animal that runs away and disappears, the bird's flight that you cannot follow, the insect that glides under stones, give birth to imaginary species, to exceptional and terrible creatures.

The Beast of Gévaudan once came rambling over these mountain regions. It must have rested its snout and its throat on the great flat rocks that overlook Sauveplane; its horned foot traced the ridges that furrow the granite of Aire de Côte and from age to age it is reborn in the imagination of the mountain and valley people. Beside it, this great apocalyptic and diabolic beast, swarm a thousand less alluring species that are almost as formidable and quite as fantastic: the viper that is smaller than a worm and kills in an instant, the wild boar that charges man and is armed like a fighting bull, the wild squirrel that attacks you like a tiger-cat, and the birds, the great birds of prey, that eat people's eyes: the eagle that is two yards long, the hawk with the iron beak, and the flocks of five hundred crows that fall in one swoop on their victim. In reality, only harmless animals feeding on carrion infest these mountains: except for the vipers that may cause instant death in hot weather, all the other beasts are helpless before man. The few remaining wolves that hide in the most secret coverts of the forest are cowardly and small in size; the wild boars flee at the least approach; and the birds of prey are content to trace great circles over the path of isolated travellers.

I have sometimes encountered carcasses on my mountain excursions. They were always rotting in severe solitude and my approach has not even stirred up a flight of flies. . . .

Just once I saw a solitary crow watching from a white rock, beside the swollen carcass of a sheep: at the sound of my steps it turned its head and flew off without regret, as if it were not used to feasting on carrion. . . .

"But," resumed Finiels, "the animals did not devour Roux the Bandit during this winter, and on the first fine days, when the people of the valley were beginning to go back to the mountain, we heard them talking about him again.

"A few woodcutters ran across him in the clearings of Luzette, and the people of the heights, coming down to the market at Saint-Jean, met him on the pass of Fauvel and talked with him for more than an hour."

I V

A T nightfall, the women came back from Saint-Jean.
Five o'clock had just sounded on the long clock, the
gilded bronze pediment of which, arranged in sheaves of
arms and flags in the style of the Directory, sparkled beside
the bread-box. The first one, the grand-daughter of Finiels,
appeared at the open door and stopped suddenly at sight of
this assembly of men grouped about her grandfather and
her father in the chimney-corner.

Behind her came the wife of Finiels, with her
daughter-in-law.

"Go in, don't stand there between our legs. You are not
afraid of people, are you?"

The two women pushed the little girl into the room
and came up to the great table, upon which they placed
the heavy baskets they had brought up from the town.
After setting down the baskets, they remained in front of
the table, their arms swinging, their heads and shoulders
thrown forward, as if still bent by the effort of the steep
climb under a double load. It was only then that we all
greeted one another, observing in this way the mountain
custom according to which we do not address one another
until we have come to a full stop, with the legs firm on the
ground and the chest freed from the breathlessness of the
ascent or the descent.

I know these two women well, but the greeting they
gave me was not the same, and a whole world of moral and
practical obligations determined its familiarity.

Finiels's wife is an old woman. She knew my grandmother well, she saw me when I was quite small, and she treats me with a sort of respectful irony, with a delicate abruptness, as if I were somewhat in her care, under her supervision, as if she felt a duty toward me.

Her daugher-in-law is a young woman whom I knew well as a young girl, seven years ago when, bold and almost insolent, she answered the pleasantries of the young men and wore green and red scarfs, the ends of which flapped in the wind against her finely cut Saracen face. We talked as good comrades in those days, and we looked each other in the eye and exchanged saucy remarks when we met on the main street of Saint-Jean or on the square by the station on Sunday evenings, while the little spinning-girls sang ballads as they waited for the ten o'clock train. But since her marriage, she no longer seems to notice the presence of young men and—like all the girls of these valleys, saucy and wanton at eighteen, then silent and discreet wives—she no longer busies herself with anything but her little daughter and her housework. . . . She will not talk with the old men until much later, when she is an old woman like her mother-in-law. Then she will regain that tone of aggressive and ironical familiarity which she had as a young girl. But there will be no longer that sensual quivering of the nostrils to animate it, those sudden movements of the lips which seem to scorn kisses. . . .

Today, her mother-in-law alone has the right to speak to us, and it is really she alone who can do it, with her mischievous authority as mistress of the house,

governess of affairs, and directress of the consciences of
the family.

While her daughter-in-law, after saluting us indifferently,
began to unpack the baskets, Finiels's wife came towards
us, and, looking at the table, which was still set, the dishes
soiled and the glasses half full, she asked Finiels in a tone
of reproach and raillery:

"You haven't let your guests starve?"

"We have eaten the beast's liver and everything that was
left in the cupboards," replied Finiels. "We also found a few
bottles and I don't think we have fared so badly. . . ."

"We shall see if they leave anything on their plates at
supper. . . . How much does it weigh?"

"Seventy-five. It is small and gave us trouble. The mayor
and the two from Bessède are still after another; they went
toward Montals, but I don't think they should be long in
coming. You can set their places; they will have supper
with us."

"So you have been out all night for nothing much,
and now you make speeches at your sweet ease. . . . Is it
Monsieur André who is talking politics?"

"It is not Monsieur André, it is I who am talking," replied
Finiels, "and I am speaking of Roux the Bandit."

"A good story to leave alone; it only makes us ashamed
and brings up regrets. . . . You don't have to make much
ado or great speeches just to tell how we spent three years
without understanding that boy's behaviour and in the end
simply had to agree with him. . . ."

"You were the first to cry out against him at the beginning of the war, and you would not even see Finette any more."

"I don't deny it: I behaved like everybody else. I must say that we had some excuse, in the first place because when a thing begins one can never properly understand it, and in the second because we had our reasons for thinking this war was different. . . . We believed it was going to make an end of all bad things, and that is why we thought everyone ought to go into it. . . . But if we had known that this war was like all the others, just good for getting people killed without changing anything, we should have said, as they said in the old days, 'Let who will go.' That was the way it was during the Crimean War, and it was the same in 1870, as my mother has told me again and again. War came, but in the country nothing changed. If there was a rascal in the valley, somebody who worked from one farm to another, without doing much, and slept in barns, he could go and seek his fortune in the army, but the others, the farming people who had their families and their regular work, remained quite peacefully at their tasks, with their families, as if there were no war. Even in 1870, when the Prussians came up to Paris and beyond, all those who set out that winter went of their own free will. Nobody was obliged to go, and whoever wished to stay behind did so. . . ."

"You would have liked everybody to refuse to go?"

"No, indeed, for we believed the war was going to change everything. But what I mean was that Roux was quite right, and that he had understood everything at once. . . . War is never a good thing, it has never led to better times for anybody. That was where we were mistaken, while he saw clearly. Now, in spite of all the misery we have been through, there are in the town well-informed and capable gentlemen, like Monsieur Rolland himself, who are already talking about the next war. . . . If it were to come back, I should like to have all the honest men climb up on the mountains together: those who were Christians would offer prayers there, and the others would talk together, like good people who do not wish ill to anybody. I can assure you, if the war begins again, I shall pack up the boy's things so that he can climb up to Aire de Côte, and I myself shall put him on the right road."

The vehemence of this old woman, the brutal decision of her words, seemed to embarrass these men. Their backs bent forward, their hands clasped and almost touching the ground, they leaned over, as if to escape from the tempest. Were they perhaps more conscious than she of the social complexity, the material difficulties, of their responsibilities? They had been soldiers, they had gone to the city, they had seen other men, commanders and judges, they felt themselves tangled in the social organism, incorporated in the nation.

Seeing them bent over in their chairs, one could not have said whether they disapproved the anger of Finiels's wife or shared it. Before these peasants of France, mountaineers of the Cévennes, loyal and sincere in character, any ringleader of men whatever might experience a pang of anxiety and doubt. The patriot who wished to call them to the national defence would probably be afraid of finding them resolutely indifferent and refractory, and the pacifist would despair of being able to lift them above their usual point of view.

Incomprehensible in the silence, they sat there, close together, watching the fire of great logs, in which the green twigs and the wet stalks were crackling.

It was, nevertheless, this question of principle, this stark problem, that aroused all their interest in the story of Roux. It was because of it that they became excited over the speeches and the adventures of this refractory soul, but, anxious to pass upon it without uncertainty, they did not wish to reach a conclusion too quickly. If they set themselves up as judges of the exigencies and institutions of men, they wished at least to respect the procedure and to safeguard all the forms while conducting the trial.

But Finiels's son broke the silence. He lifted his head, held out his hands to the fire, and in a clear voice—that businesslike voice in which he said, "Pull hard, pull to the left," when a tree was being felled, or "Hold tight" when he had to place a heavy load on the cart—he replied to his mother:

"They are not going to make us live like beasts again for five years. If there is another war I stay on the farm!"

The words fell into the silence. The most authoritative of these old mountaineers, old Finiels himself, doubtless did not feel that he had a right to contradict on this subject a young man who had fought through the whole war. They remained motionless, as if struck by the play of the great flames on the green twigs that did not catch fire easily.

Only the two sons of Liron, who had also been through the campaign, approved their comrade's words with a simple nod of the head.

Finiels's son looked at his wife and his daughter, then he turned to me and added, with that slightly distant air which he assumed only when explaining to me the details of the field work:

"You know that a peasant is made to remain on the soil. I have no desire to go running about the mountain with the *gendarmes* at my heels, trying to make me go back and fight. I must stay with my vines and my beasts, and if I have to do any shooting it will be in front of my door and at the first man who comes to tell me anything."

Finiels began talking again, but he avoided addressing his son. It was evident that he did not wish to contradict him, or even to pass sentence upon his words. So it was to his wife that he still pretended to reply, but he did not succeed in mastering a sort of awkwardness, a hesitation that seemed to trammel his gestures and his words:

"All these reasons are fine to talk about, but we did not think of them at the beginning of the war. Roux was the only one of the whole countryside who did not want to go, and if we had admitted he was right, we should have thought we were saying all the others were wrong. Besides, in order to understand him well, it was necessary for us to know his ideas, and, as I have just explained to you, we only heard them spoken of from time to time and always as things repeated by someone or other. As far as I am concerned, I have already told you that I lost all my anger with him on the day when I learned that he did not want to enlist because of his beliefs. But I continued to think he was wrong just the same, because I still had too many unanswered questions in my mind.

"You can understand this, even today, when the war is far away and men's minds turn less frequently toward these questions. When a man does not wish to fight because his beliefs forbid him, there is nothing to say, but when he refuses to share the suffering and the hardships of all men, that is another matter. I did not find any fault with Roux for not wishing to fight, but for living uselessly, like a wild beast. . . . In this connection, there was a story that went all over the countryside and gave me still more to think about.

"Perhaps you have already heard this story: it is about the pastor of Anduze, Bertin Aguillon, who went and got himself killed in the war taking care of others, and who wouldn't touch a gun or harm anyone."

I knew this story well. They had told it to me again and again in the evenings, at the time of the autumn reunions. The wounded soldiers spread it about the country during the first months of 1915: repeated by all the old people of the high valleys, it immediately entered the cycle of the moral tales of the mountain. It soon took on the aspect of a legend because, with the actual fact of the death and the official reports, there were mingled the mysterious

ANDRÉ CHAMSON

interpretations of simple souls. . . . Now the little Protestant communities of the Cévennes have finally received it into their golden legend of the martyrs and confessors of the gospel: humble tales that will never emerge from the narrow circle in which they were born and which are very often nothing but family traditions accepted by a few neighbouring families. . . .

With a nod, I indicated to Finiels that I knew this story, and, while he went on with his tale, I admired silently the sureness with which the similitudes and comparisons were brought about in his mind. The story of Roux and that of the pastor of Anduze seemed in fact to compose two parallel lives centring about the same problem and each offering a different answer. But this identity, more subtle than that of the parallel lives of antiquity, could only be felt by an intelligence habituated to weighing the problems of the conduct of life. Without any effort and through a natural application of his taste for morality, Finiels had understood the lesson that the comparison of these two stories offered.

"Since you know the story of the pastor of Anduze, you will understand all the ideas it put into my head. This pastor had had, at bottom, the same ideas as Roux, but he had put them into practice in another way, and so well that everybody was obliged to do homage to him. So I wondered if Roux could find an excuse for himself if he were faced with this man. . . . To tell the truth, I didn't believe it, but, before considering the thing as certain, I wanted to hear what he would say for himself in his own defence. I felt sure that I should meet him some day or other on the mountain, and I was awaiting this day to make up my mind finally about his behaviour. . . .

"As I had thought, I ran across him; at the beginning of the spring of 1916, near Roquelongue, one day when I had gone to gather a little bundle of faggots.

"I was still up above the meadows when night began to fall: the wind drove the fog from Luzette and whirled about my bundle as if it were going to throw me into the valley. On that side, the short cuts are steep, and it is a bad place to go down by. . . . One false step and you would go rolling into the depths of Roquelongue.

"So I stopped a few minutes on the Col du Pas for a breathing space. As I was getting ready to set off again, I saw a man come out of the forest and walk toward me: it was Roux. His clothes were all torn by the brambles, and he had a canvas bag over his shoulder and a long beard that reached to the middle of his chest. He was thinner, and he bent over more than before his misconduct, but he had a more determined air, as if, in the meantime, he had become the head of a family, with burdens and authority.

"We wished each other good evening, and Roux came and sat down near me on the grass. I said to him:

" 'The winter was bitter.'

" 'Still bitterer on the mountain than in the valley.'

"At that, I looked at him without answering, and for two minutes we did not know what more to say.

"But during this silence, I turned everything over in my mind and tried to find a way of making him explain his behaviour.

" 'Roux, the pastor of Anduze has been killed in the war. He did not want to fight, either, because of conscientious reasons. But he went just the same, like the others, in order not to put himself in the wrong. When he reached his regiment, he went to find his colonel and told him that his conscience forbade him to fight, but that it commanded him to go and care for the wounded, in the most dangerous places. The colonel listened to him. Nobody made any trouble for him, and he set out with the others, but without taking a gun. In the campaign, he shared the sufferings of those who were fighting, he even comforted them by being always in the thickest part of the first line in order to pick up those who were struck, and he ended by being struck himself and dying, while still giving a good example of courage and calmness to all who were near him and who also were exposed to death from one moment to another.'

"I had struck the right note. Roux the Bandit had listened to me, bending toward me as if he had been stunned by my words.

"It was more than a year since the pastor had been killed, but Roux had not yet heard of it and his ignorance was understandable, for he had not talked with more than five or six persons, and they had quite enough to do questioning him and talking to him about the people of our valley, without trying to give him the news of the whole countryside. If I told him this story, it was because I had an idea in the back of my mind, and you must know what it was. . . .

"Thus Roux the Bandit remained as if stunned by the news. You would have said he had just learned that some misfortune had befallen a member of his family. I don't know whether he was whispering a prayer, or whether he could not collect himself, but he remained all of two minutes without saying anything, half-bending toward me, his face deeply agitated. Then, after a moment, he made an effort to collect himself and asked me to tell him the story in detail.

"Whereupon I took up the story again, explaining to him everything you know: the decision of the pastor not to fight, his departure as a hospital-attendant, his devotion to the soldiers, and his calm death in the midst of battle. I repeated to him everything the men on furlough had told us about this death and the good example it had set them; I repeated to him also the last words of the pastor, who had sent a message to his wife, asking her to teach his son to detest war. . . . When I had finished this story, Roux said to me:

" 'He was an upright man. . . . He has set the best example in this war.'

" 'If he has set the best example, you would have done well to follow him instead of running off to the mountain.'

"Roux the Bandit looked at me, his right hand resting on his thigh and his left hand holding the cord of his bag. Then he said:

" 'A pastor should always watch over the flock. If the flock goes astray and is in danger of the precipices, the pastor should follow it just the same. If sickness falls on the flock, the pastor should take care of it and remain near it, even though the sickness be carried by flies or by the air which it poisons. And as long as men make war, the pastors cannot refuse to go, because they must be wherever there is suffering and misfortune. Into the midst of war they can carry the good Word, as the pastor of Anduze was able to do. . . . But the duty of the Christian is not the same. He may refuse to follow the flock that goes astray, he is not obliged to accompany it in all its tribulations.'

"Then, as if to explain to me what he had just said, Roux added in another voice:

" 'Come, Finiels, you must remember that before the war there was a pastor in the town who did a great deal of good. I loved to hear him talk and I would have made real sacrifices for that man, so that I never missed one of his sermons. . . .

" 'You may have heard it said that this pastor often went into the bad cafés in Nimes and Alais, to talk to those who were misbehaving and paid no heed to the Word. Well, in spite of all the pleasure I took in listening to him, if people had told me to follow him into those evil places, I must have replied that it was not my business, and I would have refused to listen to them.'

"This was well said and I realised that Roux's reason was worth something. But I had still more to say to him when he forestalled me and said:

" 'I know quite well that if war is an evil thing, those who are forced to wage it are yet honest according to their sense of honesty. In saying what I have just said, I do not mean to compare them with those who live wretched lives, but to explain that the first duty of the pastor was to follow the misery of men. My duty was not the same; it was—not to risk killing my neighbour. . . .'

" 'You could have enlisted just the same, refusing to fight and asking to take care of the others. . . . They certainly allowed the pastor to do so.'

" 'Yes, but the pastor was a clever man and his commanders listened to him because of this. If I gave myself up, I would have had to go like the others: a peasant cannot reason with city gentlemen. They respected the pastor's determination, but they would have done violence to my own, and nobody, neither the colonel nor the government, would even have listened to me.'

"That was a real reason, Monsieur André, and I found myself at once of Roux's opinion. . . . You cannot deny it: when he is up against the government, a peasant must do everything that is asked of him, without discussing it, or else refuse to do it altogether."

Finiels was going to speak further, but the door opened suddenly and the mayor, followed by the two boys from Bessède, entered the room.

"How much does she weigh?" Finiels cried out to them amid a burst of laughter.

"She weighs more than yours, but she is still running," replied the mayor, seating himself near us.

"If you had not left, we would surely have got it, but there were not enough of us to place a guard on all the trails. . . ."

"We might all have stayed all night on the mountain without seeing her," replied Finiels's son. "I told you that at about eight o'clock the dogs had taken the wrong back-scent, and I am quite sure you did not even hear them give tongue for her."

"Yes, indeed," said the elder of the boys from Bessède, "we heard them pick up her scent in the Calles de Grimald, and they followed her in full cry as far as the plateau. She passed like lightning a hundred yards away from me and in my excitement I fired my gun at her twice. It was a fine animal, larger than the one Finiels killed this morning, and it snorted like an ox. The dogs were not able to round it up. There were not enough of them. . . . You might at least have left us yours. . . ."

V

THE hunting stories, the technical discussions, and the long controversies that sometimes kept us passionately interested for hours, could not hold us today. The sound of the wind on the shutters, the wavering of the night fogs before the door, the damp and tenacious odour of the high meadows which enveloped the last comers, all those things that come from the mountain and recall it, and especially the presence of Finiels, led our thoughts back to the story of Roux. We could not make up our minds to talk of anything else with interest or even with indifference. The mayor and the two boys from Bessède did not, for that matter, try to continue the story of their hunt: tired out from the long chase, they accepted our gibes and our raillery, happy to let their wet gaiters steam before the fire and to stretch out to the flame their hands, which were red and rough like bricks. On our part, we did not attempt to drag out our pleasantries, to connect them with fresh stories of unfortunate hunts, to support them by grotesque anecdotes, as we are accustomed to do on the mountain; but we turned toward Finiels and our silence seemed to leave the talk to him. Finiels knew what we wanted, but he appeared to hesitate to continue his story; he was silent for several minutes, then suddenly he decided to speak:

"I am going to finish telling my story . . . with the permission of the mayor and the government."

We all began to laugh as we looked at the mayor, who smiled also, but who did not understand this sally. At first I thought it only a jest of good-natured familiarity, but, looking at Finiels closely, I noticed in him an element of distrust and perhaps even of hostility.

"I was speaking of Roux," added Finiels, with the same air of aggressive embarrassment.

The mayor just shrugged his shoulders, while the two boys from Bessède sat motionless on their chairs, attentive like all the other mountaineers.

"I had reached the next to the last year of the war," resumed Finiels, "or, if you prefer, the year 1917. During the good season of that year, Roux the Bandit made a slight change in his quarters: he forsook the slopes of Sauveplane for those of Lingas, on account of Birenque, the shepherd of Dourbies, who passed the summer on the meadows of this mountain with three or four flocks which they brought up to him from the lowlands in the hot weather.

"This Birenque was very much in need of a little help to get through all his work. When a sheep was injured and another was lost, he was obliged to set out in two directions at once. As Roux was wandering about the mountain, with nothing to occupy him, the least he could do was to try to make himself useful. Two or three times he chanced to find a lost sheep and bring it back to Birenque. To reward him Birenque made him share his daily food, and gradually, although they never shook hands on a mutual agreement, they formed the habit of staying together: Roux the Bandit watched Birenque's sheep and Birenque shared his dinner with Roux.

"This Birenque was a half-crazy old man, the one who made up songs and who died last year. He knew all about his sheep and his dance tunes, but as for anything else, he lived as if nothing else existed. . . . He knew just what to do when it concerned music, and, if making songs could be called a trade, one might say that Birenque was a good workman. He made his music first: music for dancing almost always, or sometimes music for singing as you walked—bringing in the cattle, for instance. When he had found his music, he delighted in putting the words to it, then he went about singing his songs on the farms and in the villages.

"You must know his songs: the girls must have taught them to you. At least you know this one. . . ."

And Finiels hummed softly, to a mountain air, these words which I knew well:

> *T'aimo b'un paou, mioune,*
> *Mai pa gaire:*
> *T'aimo b'un paou, mioune,*
> *Un paou mai pa gaire;*
> *T'aimo pa pus*
> *Ai conneigut l'abus. . . .*

---

* I love you a little, my own, but not much, I love you a little, my own, a little but not much; I do not love you more, because I have known [your] abuse.

How could I be ignorant of this song? It was to this that the mountain girls had danced at the village fêtes ever since the end of the war. Marcelle and Noélie had taught it to me, and I had seen them dancing their *raïole* borée while they sang it. They had assured me that it was indeed composed by a shepherd of Dourbies, but I had not believed them. For if the music of this borée had the cadence of all the mountain refrains—with something more strained, more ironical perhaps—its words seemed to me so pure, so perfect, that it was impossible for me not to pay homage to the most ancient and the most refined basis of the folklore of the high valleys. I believed that it required a great number of successive versions, and the slow labour of inattentive but subtle minds, skilful in modifying words and measures, to give so finished a perfection to any songs which the shepherds might compose. But I no longer had the right to doubt, for Finiels assured me that this song was the work of Birenque and that, before they had heard him sing it at the fêtes of Espérou, Camprieu, and Dourbies, nobody in the whole country could have said the first line of it.

"He has made a good many others, Monsieur André, and longer ones. He has even made some that would make you think he had something in his mind, and yet, I repeat, he was a simpleton and apart from his songs one could never get anything out of him.

"The people of the upper slopes, who knew that he had spent whole days with Roux, told him whenever he came down to the village for his provisions:

" 'Watch out, Birenque, the *gendarmes* will put you in prison at the same time as the boy from Sauveplane.'

"And Birenque could only reply:

" 'The boy lives near, and doesn't mind giving me a hand. I could not repay him by throwing stones at him.'

"This was doubtless Roux's happiest time on the mountain. It was still a difficult time, for he had to sleep on the ground with a flint under his head, but at last, although it was no feast, he had almost enough to eat every day and he was no longer alone with the wild beasts, and with no one to talk to.

"My boy, who had leave of absence at this period, always answered with a laugh, when people spoke to him about Roux:

" 'The monster is taking his time of rest with Birenque.'

"He did not say this as a reproach. Quite on the contrary. Besides, I have never heard anybody—either the old people of this region or the men passing on leave—wish Roux's bad times to begin again. But this peace was not made to last, and all the misfortunes of the boy were coming back of themselves.

"After the first heavy autumn rain, Birenque closed his hut, herded his beasts together, and returned to the lowlands. With the bad weather, Roux the Bandit again found himself all alone on the mountain.

"He could not think of remaining on the plain of Lingas because that is one of the worst spots on the mountain during the winter season, and certainly the most solitary, for you have to go down to the bottom of the valley to find a village or even a farm that is inhabited the whole year round.

"So he returned to Luzette on account of his mother and all the people he knew who lived on the farms under this shoulder of the mountain. Our countryside is less deserted than the plain of Lingas, and, by remaining thus in the retired parts of Luzette, Roux did not have too long a road to travel to get provisions. You know that he had already had to manage this way during the three winters he had spent on the mountain, and during this last bad season of the war it was still easier for him to get along, since nobody was angry with him any more.

"There wasn't a man left in the whole valley who thought of betraying Roux, or even giving him a harsh word. Gradually, we all persuaded ourselves that he could not go to the war, and it was almost as if he had been discharged by the government. Of course we knew that he could not have been discharged for lack of arms or legs, but we allowed ourselves to believe that he might have been discharged because of the ideas he had, and it seemed to us all that this, too, was a good excuse.

"At this time, if Roux had wished to made an end of his privations and go into hiding on a farm, it would certainly not have been difficult. All the corn-lofts in the neighbourhood of Sauveplane and Bessède would have been opened to him; plenty of people would have managed to place a mattress and blankets for him in a corner of their silk-worm nursery or their orchard."

"That would not have been too easy," broke in the mayor, "for the *gendarmes* have eyes and they would not have permitted this boy to spend the winter in warmth and comfort while all the men of his age were going to war."

"If Roux had wished to hide on a farm, the *gendarmes* would have know nothing about it, for nobody would have come to betray him," replied Finiels, "and this would have been right, for, after all, the boy was not dishonest and he was harming nobody."

"We agree on that. . . . He was not dishonest, but, all the same, in allowing him to live at peace in the very midst of the war they would have set too bad an example."

"A bad example? But to whom? All the young men of our families were in the war, and since, from the first, they had not behaved like Roux, they had no reason for changing their behaviour after having seen four years of campaigning."

"I am not speaking for you or yours, Finiels, I know quite well that you always act honestly and according to your beliefs, but everybody is not like you, and there are people who are always ready to follow the worst example."

"They always say that. It is a plan of government to talk about those who are not honest to prevent those who are honest from doing the most natural things. . . . But how can you speak thus of those who are not honest? You know very well that there are not many of them in our country (three or four, here and there) and that, apart from them, you can answer for everybody. . . . So there was no question of setting a bad example, but simply of having pity for an unfortunate man. That is why Roux would have had no trouble finding a hiding-place. Moreover, don't let me say that he could have gone and hidden anywhere; there were plenty of farms where they would not have been willing to take him in, especially those where there were women with husbands or sons in the war. I say merely that he would have had no difficulty in finding a farm where people would have welcomed him, without saying anything to anyone. But this boy was not like most folk: he was not looking out for his own comfort or even seeking an end to his miseries. He resigned himself, indeed, to coming to get a bit of bread and cheese from people, but he would go back to the mountain at once, in the midst of the snow and the bad weather. It was like an unchangeable determination or a fixed idea, a sort of need to escape from comfort and make himself suffer.

"Very often, at this period, Roux came to the farms on our side of the mountain, toward nightfall. The people took him in as if he had been a travelling salesman: they gave him a plate of warm soup which he ate immediately and a bit of bread and stew which he stowed away in his knapsack, and then, whether it snowed or rained, he set out again for the mountain without their being able to keep him for the night.

"Once, I recall, when the deep winter was setting in, I had gone up for the evening to see my cousins the Perriers. Their boy had come home on leave and we wanted to have a little chat together.

"It was a time of bad weather, at the change of the moon, ice and snow and pitch-black night over the whole countryside. As always, the bad weather came down from Luzette, and yet, in this darkness, Luzette showed as a white spot: the deep snow came down all the way to the meadows of Roquelongue, and the ice had covered the *fangas** of the Méjean farm, the ground of which shone like fragments of broken glass. . . . You know the sort of weather.

"As we were finishing supper, crowded about the fire as we are here, Roux arrived. He came now and then to this farm where the people were kind to him, because of a daughter who had married some relative of his. I had not seen him since spring, but he was still just the same, with his disgraceful clothes, his great wild beard, and his long hair. Seeing him, you would have said he was an animal, or that man of wax which they showed me once in the museum at Nîmes, in front of a cave, with a stone axe in his hand. But when he spoke he was a man like you and me.

"He said good day to everybody, without embarrassment and without surprise, then he went and sat down near the fireplace. The women brought him some soup and warm wine. He ate his soup, not ravenously like a hungry man who gobbles one mouthful after another, but, on the contrary, like someone who reflects as he performs an important act.

* "Marshy land, mire; rich, damp soil."—Mistral, *Lou Tresor dou Felibrige.*

"While he was eating, the women filled his knapsack with bread and home-made sausage. We all looked at him without speaking, and the soldier more than the rest of us, and as if the desire to speak to him were on the tip of his tongue. . . .

"When he had finished his soup, Roux set his plate down and looked at the soldier. The soldier was still looking at him, and we wondered what they were going to say to each other.

"Outside was the tumult of the storm. The *pansière** of the Perriers, which is behind the farm of my cousins, just below their terrace, made a terrible noise in the sluices of the mill. Every minute you might have thought that the conduit had been suddenly stopped up and that it was going to be carried away, and that half the river was hurling itself over it, as if all the water of the mountain had come down at once.

"In the end, Roux and the soldier began to talk. We had thought they were going to discuss the war, but, on the contrary, they began discussing the work of the countryside. . . . The soldier was anxious about his little vineyard at the bottom of the hill which is just beside mine and which he had planted a short time before the war.

" 'It had a fine start,' he said. 'The soil of this land is good although it is a little light. I have sent for the plans of Vezénobre, and I have more than five terraces.'

* Dam, dike, causeway for raising water. In *langue d'oc* "pansiero."

" 'The best wine in the country is made on that mountain,' replied Roux, 'but it is not heavy enough, and if you don't take care it turns more quickly than you can drink it.'

" 'That is true of the lowlands, but not of our villages. At Nîmes they can't keep this wine, even in the best cellars. . . . We know something about it because of our cousins at Mont-du-Plan who carried away a little keg of it and were not able to drink it. But on the mountain this wine can be kept well and it can even become especially good, because of the height. . . .'

" 'That's true, nowhere save at Sauveplane does the wine keep better than at Bessède or Saint-Jean. I remember how my poor father had a little cask of wine that was beginning to turn brought up to Bessède. Everybody laughed when they saw him take such pains, but after it had stayed quietly in our cellar for six months, this bad wine was just as good as Tavel or the light wines they harvest in the neighbourhood of Uzès.'

"Thus Roux and the soldier talked, as if there had not been any war, as if Roux had not committed any act of folly. Presently Roux got up, took his knapsack, and slung it over his shoulder. My cousin, who saw that Roux wanted to go, went to the door and looked out at the weather.

"The snow entered the open door with one of those gusts of wind on a level with the ground that lash your legs and bend you in two. At the same moment a great mass of water leaped over the *pansière* and made a whirlpool under the little wall of the terrace. My cousin closed the door and said to Roux:

" 'You are not going out in this storm. Put down your knapsack and stay with us.'

"But Roux would not listen to him, and said good-bye to everybody. As we were all telling him to stay, he answered that he had to go back to the mountain and that he had already stayed with us too long.

" 'To everybody his own destiny. I must spend the winter on Luzette. . . .'

"We were not able to do anything with him and Roux set off again in the storm. He took the path that climbed up to Roquelongue following the river of the country, and that night, as on many another, he went and slept in one of the grottos of Luzette, where he had nothing better than a bed of branches. . . .

"I did not see him again all that winter, which was as bad as the rest. . . . In our mountains, winter is always winter, and when one speaks of past times there's always the same thing to say about the three or four bad months of snow. But what really changes, what is never the same from one year to another, is the spring. . . . This year, our spring was open as on the plain: it did not drag out in the Rouergue and we did not have a single late frost. From the first the roads were firm and the snow melted and the trees bloomed. Summer weather, but summer without drought. The spring water, which is better than that of the other seasons, ran everywhere, in the meadows, in the gardens, in the basins of the terraces. . . . It was a blue water that exhaled the odour of snow and sunlight, a water that brought results.

"With this spring, Roux came roaming more and more about the farms and villages. Now that it was good weather on the mountain, he did not seem to want to stay there particularly. But at the same time that he became less wary, the *gendarmes* began to make things worse for him. During this fine weather, they did not go on their rounds so regularly: you saw them one day at Bessède, the next day at Mouzoules, the day after toward Sauveplane. They had received new orders from the city, or perhaps they were angry with themselves, feeling that all the people had become comrades of Roux the Bandit.

"For several months they obliged Roux to hide in the woods behind Luzette. Only at night was he able to resume his wandering toward the villages. The dogs never barked at him, for he was a familiar figure at all the farms, all the sheepfolds."

"That is true," resumed the oldest of the boys from Bessède, "our two dogs, which are worse than all the others in the valley taken together, never stirred when Roux passed by our door. And this was not natural, for dogs like ours bark at the least suspicion and at anything that is out of the way. From the valley to the mountain, they feel everything strange or unwonted that happens. . . . When one evening, after a storm, a gully that had never had water began to flow for a few hours down across our farm, ravaging the garden-plots of the terraces, the dogs howled all the time. . . ."

"Which proves that Roux did nothing wrong on the mountain, and that his presence there was natural, like that of a good spring which always flows. . . .

"At this period, when Roux was out walking in the night, he often met people he knew, mountain folk who were late in returning to their homes. He spoke to them and helped them carry the sacks which they were bringing up from the town. It was always at late hours, toward the middle of the night, for Roux did not dare leave the woods before ten o'clock, because of the *gendarmes,* who now and then made their rounds in our villages at that hour. . . .

"This surveillance prevented him from coming to eat with the people of the farm, as he had done in the winter, at the time when the *gendarmes* did not come up to the mountain; now when he reached the villages all the doors were closed and people had been sleeping for a long time. Therefore, in order that he might not risk dying of hunger, the women on the farm in the neighbourhood of Roquelongue or behind Le Pas, toward Mouzoules, very often, in the evening, left something to eat on the little walls of their terraces. And when Roux the Bandit passed, late at night, on his way down from the mountain, he would take a bit of bread and cheese which they had left for him in front of the door.

"Little by little, this had become a habit of the mountain folk and almost a superstition; many women would not have been willing to go to sleep any more, or throw the ashes over the logs or even put away their dishes and set the room in order, without having prepared the provisions for Roux, for they somehow believed that this would bring them good fortune."

The elder of the boys from Bessède could not remain motionless on his chair. He rocked himself to right and left, then suddenly, as if to force himself to remain quiet, he bent forward, leaned his elbows on his knees, stretched out his forearms and joined his hands, in a nervous gesture of passionate attention. Like all the other mountaineers, he followed ardently Finiels's story, but he was not satisfied to follow it in silence, he had to share in it also, and this ardour, which drove him to remain last on the mountain on hunting days, seemed to animate him still and obliged him to emphasise all the passages of any importance, to uphold by his testimony all the facts that might seem doubtful.

"That is the truth," he said, "and I know it well, for I was at home the last year of the war on account of my leg and a bursting shell. At Borie they always left Roux's share outside the door; they placed it on the highest end of the terrace wall so that the beasts couldn't get at it, and always in the same plate—'Roux's plate,' as my aunt said. And even well after the end of the war, when Roux had been in prison for a long time, there still were women who wanted to leave something to eat outside the door, they had been so accustomed to doing this every evening and it had been such a great pleasure."

"True," said Finiels, "but just as in other years, the *gendarmes* ended by tiring themselves out. They climbed up to the mountain less often, as if they were discouraged or as if Roux were no longer there. . . . Then Roux sometimes came down earlier, and toward the close of summer, as he knew the days when the *gendarmes* were watching the other side of the valley, near the main stream, he even ended by coming down to our villages in the afternoon. He stopped and talked with the people whom he met on the terraces, who were working the soil, and often he even lent them a hand."

"Yes," said the boy from Bessède, "he helped us in our grape-gathering just a few days before he was taken by the *gendarmes*. . . . At Bessède, we do not gather the grapes very early, but at the end of September, and when the bad weather has already begun. Ours are not pleasant harvestings such as they have on the plain. We begin them in the sun and finish them in the rain and fog. And the moment the grapes are ripe, we make as much haste as possible: but this year we didn't have enough people; we were four, all told, for the harvesting; my father, my two sisters, and I. And I was still limping. There were just enough of us to manage the cart. My father and my elder sister carried the baskets and my other sister was left alone to do the cutting. . . . On the morning of the harvesting, we climbed up to the vineyard. The weather was threatening, the Cap de Coste was in fog, and the valley of Calles was entirely covered. . . ."

Finiels's son thought he should add to this description of the weather the proverb which has established its meteorological significance for the inhabitants of these mountains. For every aspect of the horizon there is a corresponding proverb, and all these proverbs compose a sort of rose of the winds, in consecutive rhymes.

> *"Quand lou cap de Costo mes soun capel*
> *Lou pastre pòu mestre soun mantel."* *

"Quite true," concluded the boy from Bessède, "but just the same, while we were waiting for the storm, the sun came out from the other side, from the direction of Séranne, and burned our backs. 'Not for twenty hectogrammes of grapes,' said my father, 'did I come out to catch a cold on my chest.'

"We had scarcely begun to work when Roux leaped into the midst of the four of us: he came down from the mountain through the terraces.

" 'You come in good time to give us a little help,' my father said to him.

" 'It is always pleasant work gathering grapes,' replied Roux.

" 'But it's a bad business, just the same, carrying the baskets,' my sister said to him, laughing.

" 'Good,' said Roux. 'I'll carry the baskets. . . . That is no work for women.'

---

* When the Cap de Coste puts on its cap, the shepherd can put on his cloak.

"Naturally, I had not seen Roux since the beginning of the war. I did not know what to say to him: I was not angry with him, for you cannot be angry with people who act according to their beliefs, when they are not insincere . . . but Finiels has told you this better than I.

"So I held the mule by the bridle, at the entrance to the vineyard, when my father, seeing that we embarrassed each other, bethought himself to say:

" 'The boy hasn't got the whole use of his leg.'

" 'All right,' said Roux. 'Don't let him tire himself; when I have carried the baskets, I shall go down with the cart as far as the good road.'

"But I answered: 'I can walk all right, alongside the mule. So long as it is not too much, I can do anything. . . .'

" 'If you prefer,' said Roux to me, 'I will do the cutting and carry the baskets, the work will go more quickly. . . . All these aramons will spoil if they are wet by the storm. . . .'

"All day, Roux worked with us as if he had been labouring at fixed wages. Only at noon we had a bite to eat and Roux with us, but we did not talk much because the weather was more and more threatening. Toward four o'clock, when it began to rain, we were just finishing our harvesting. Roux came down with us as far as the good road, for he wanted to lead the mule, which took fright at the thunder and was not easy to hold. . . .

"When we reached the road, he left us without saying much of anything, but as my father was thanking him again for his help:

" 'It is as if the other boy were here,' he replied, as he went off.

"He meant my brother who was at Salonica with the Fortieth."

"This was not the only piece of help which he gave people who were working on the mountain," resumed Finiels, "and, indeed, it was this that undid him. At the beginning of October, he stayed several days with the woodcutters in the woods of Luzette, making up little bundles of faggots and bringing them down by the cable.

"I remember that one day I was passing along the road of Grenouillet just where the cable comes down from Roque-Pertuse. At the foot of the cable, I found the farmer of Vernède with his boy. They were receiving beech faggots and putting them into their cart. I asked them:

" 'Have you a workman on the mountain?'

"They began to laugh.

" 'A good journeyman, who understands the work very well. No fear, with him, that the faggots will slide into one another.'

"I looked at the cable. The bundles of faggots were coming down one after another, at regular intervals. They rushed down, whistling in the air like a stone, and struck against the *butoir* of the cable. The boy from Vernède had just time to free his bundle when the next one arrived in its turn—and so on, without stopping for a minute. Seeing the work going this way, anyone would have known that it was no green hand who was loading the cable.

"The two men were still laughing—then the father said to me:

" 'It's Roux who is on the mountain. He made up the bundles with us and now he is sending them down to us.'

"From above—a hundred metres in the air on the edge of Roque-Pertuse—the bundles of wood were still gliding down. I watched them descending on the cable, and I felt joy in my heart at the thought that Roux was working at his trade, being of service to somebody, earning his right to live. . . .

"From that time he ventured more and more into the lower parts of the valley, working here and there when he found work to do. And people allowed themselves to talk about it and repeated it in the villages.

"All this tittle-tattle came back to the *gendarmes*, not through malevolence, but rather through the stupidity of this, that, and the other. You see, there are men who do not know how to hold their tongues: when they come down to Saint-Jean the café-keepers get them to babble out all the gossip of the mountain. I heard them say: 'Roux has taken up his old trade again. . . .' And more of the same.

"So, on the second Tuesday in October, we were getting ready to go out for chestnuts. This was just the day when the *gendarmes* were in the habit of making their rounds toward the river, and we did not think they were on our side of the mountain.

"We had been all day getting the frames ready for the blankets when, toward five o'clock, they came to tell me that the *gendarmes* had taken Roux below Mouzoules. . . . The village was in a turmoil, and all the people gathered to discuss the news.

"We did not want to believe it. It seemed to us that Roux was no longer at fault, that the *gendarmes* no longer had any concern with him. But you may imagine that what we thought had nothing to do with the matter. When the *gendarmes* make trouble for men who go fishing, for those who do not light the lanterns on their carts, for those who cut wood in the forest, we do not think them right. On the contrary, we think them wrong for not putting in prison those who make scandal, hypocrisy, and spite. . . . But, for all that, they have their orders and we can't do anything about it.

"It was true that the *gendarmes* had taken Roux the Bandit below Mouzoules. They had lain in wait for him for more than half an hour while he talked with two men who were watching their sheep in the little meadow that slopes up to the notch. When he had come down to the road, they seized him without any difficulty, and then they went straight to Saint-Jean by the short cuts and without letting anyone see them.

"How had the *gendarmes* guessed where Roux was? I can't tell you, but some say that it was the little girl from Mouzoules who betrayed him. This child, who was not yet twelve years old, had gone to the spring on the road to get a jug of fresh water. In passing through the meadows, she had seen Roux with the two shepherds of Mouzoules. . . .

She may indeed have repeated it to the *gendarmes,* but with no thought of harm.

"Now this girl is grown up. She is even old enough to be married, but nobody looks at her—it is as if there were a curse upon her. . . . They don't blame her perhaps, but they avoid her like one who is marked for evil. . . ."

"I am not going to speak to her," said the boy from Bessède, "no matter how she flirts."

"As for the end of the story, I can't tell you much. From Saint-Jean they sent Roux to the town, then they put him on trial. He was not sentenced until after the armistice, and all we know is that he kept saying over and over that they could kill him but he would kill nobody. . . . They sentenced him to jail for twenty years: he stayed some time in the prison at Nîmes, then they sent him to another prison on the seashore, in the neighbourhood of Bordeaux. It seems that he is loved by everybody in that prison. . . ."

"Yes, and they have even made him some sort of an assistant guard, under the regular wardens, because of his courage and intelligence."

It was the wife of Finiels who, from the end of the room, added this testimony to the words of her husband. Since the arrival of the mayor, she had kept apart, but from the way she handled the dishes and the pots I had felt her there, uncompromising, nervous, and always attentive to what her husband was saying.

"They have not been too hard on him," said the mayor. "For a boy of thirty, twenty years in prison won't reach to the end of his life. He can keep the hope of ending his days in his own home. . . ."

"It would be better for him to come back at once. His mother and his sister Amélie are waiting for him; there are only two of them left to take care of the farm, and if nobody comes to their help the soil of Sauveplane will have become a waste again, in twenty years. . . .

"The elder sister is not at Sauveplane any more," resumed Finiels, responding to the gesture of astonishment I had just made, "and this, with all the details, would make another long story. . . . But we are not going to tell love-stories now.

"When the war broke out the girl was about to marry a boy who did carting over by Saint-Etienne. This Bertin had to go, like the rest, and at first his family would no longer hear of the marriage, because of Roux. You can imagine the hard time the girl went through.

"Like her mother and her sister Amélie, she had to suffer the insolence of people because of her brother's act of folly. But she suffered still more in her feelings, forsaken as she was.

"Bertin left her without news for more than a year, then they wrote each other a few letters, and on one of his periods of leave he went up as far as Sauveplane. . . . He wanted to make up with her, but his father, who is a patriot, with medals from several campaigns, and a sergeant in the Colonials, would not hear of it. There was a terrible quarrel between Roux's sister, this boy, and his family, and always a bad time for the girl. . . . Little by little, things quieted down, and after the war they were married just the same, without any special celebration, as if the family had been in mourning: and the sister left Sauveplane and came to live at Saint-Etienne. . . .

"Her mother and the other sister have remained all alone on the mountain, and this is a great pity, because they are not equal to the work on their hands and every year the undergrowth creeps in and swallows up a little more.

"Farms like that need strong arms. They have been taken by force from the mountain and the mountain lies in wait all the time to take them back.

"My great-grandfather saw the time when Sauveplane was only a sheepfold and a waste. The Rouxs and the Trézics made a good property of it, and in the middle of the last century it was almost a village, with three farms, several barns, a spring, and reservoirs. On its threshing-floor they threshed more wheat than was needed for three families. They brought down cheeses, butter, and chestnuts: during the winter they made sabots, collars, and little bells for the sheep. They married and children were born there.

"Now it is poverty-stricken. Of the three families there remains only an old woman and one unmarried girl. The reservoirs have filled up with mud, the ploughed lands have become as hard as stone, the chestnut-trees that have died have not been replaced, and the great farm itself, the one they called in my father's time 'l'Oustau Nou,'* has begun to decay.

* The New House.

"You can climb up to Sauveplane and see the desolation of that valley! The wild places on the mountain that have never been tilled are not melancholy: solitude is natural to them. But abandoned fields, where one sees the old traces of cultivation, are a sorrier sight than the cemeteries. . . ."

"You have told enough of this story," resumed Finiels's wife. "It is supper-time. I am going to set the table, but you had better go and take a turn on the terrace and let me sweep up. You have brought in all the mud of the Méjean farm on your gaiters. . . ."

We all rose. Finiels's son and the two boys from Bessède went ahead.

"I am going to see the dogs. . . . Bombarde has hurt her paw, going through the brambles."

The mayor and Panard went out also. I remained alone in the room with Finiels: we went slowly toward the door. The evening sky seemed to rest on the rim of the terrace, the fog rose toward it from the neighbouring slopes. Bombarde whimpered softly from the barn.

I understood that Roux's story was finished, that Finiels had nothing more to say and did not wish to say anything more. But if, when he began his story, I was content to imagine the physical appearance of his hero, I now desired to know exactly how his face looked and what was his bearing.

"I must have known this Roux of Sauveplane before the war, but I can't recall him. . . ."

"He was a man much like everybody else: in person a little like my boy, a little like the boys from Bessède. Not too tall, but slightly stooped. . . . He wore a moustache, but no beard, at least before the war, for while he was in hiding he allowed his hair to grow all over, as I have told you. . . . But this beard was of no importance, for his eyes made up his whole face: great blue eyes with a kind of sadness in them. . . . His face was long and a little pointed, and his cheeks seemed to meet at the chin, which gave him an attentive air, as if he were always listening to something. . . .

"How is he now? I cannot tell you, but it is certain that in twenty years he will be an old man, like me, with arms too long and legs a little bent. . . ."

Looking at Finiels, I complete this description, and without effort phrases are born in me that add themselves to his phrases and seem to compose a portrait full of proud justice:

These arms, too long from having held too many short-handled tools, these legs bent from having walked on both sides of the furrows and over rough land, and especially this face where the striking, the essential thing is the line of the hair, straight and black and parallel with the line of the eyebrows, and which seems to express a tenacious rectitude, an integrity that knows no compromise.